Butch

Kris Renee

A Note From The Author

Butch came to me in a dream.

I know, I know - but don't give up on me yet! Just hear me out!

You're probably thinking, "Come on Kris, that is so cliche!" And you're not wrong! I know we've all heard the whole *"I had a dream about it"* before. But I really truly did have an honest to goodness dream about Butch Casady!

The dream came to me right after Christmas and New Years celebrations were wrapping up. I was in the throes of writing Dark Succession and promoting The False Villain. I was still crafting on television weekly in Cleveland and creating content for my television show Craft Table. Add all that in with my everyday life as a mother of eight, and you could say I had a *lot* going on.

Now, what's crazy about the whole gosh darn thing (other than a steamy fictional guy talking to me in my head all. the. time.) is that when I first began my writing journey, I was confident that I'd be writing fantasy romance and historical romance since that is primarily what I have read over the past twenty years or so. Moreso on the "historical" side because it's where I felt safe.

So when I woke up after having my "dream about dreamy Butch", I grabbed my phone, opened up my *Notes* app, and recorded the handful of details that I could remember. And I could remember quite a lot, actually. Unlike most of my dreams, there were a lot of specifics floating around for me to grab and hold onto. I typed them all out in the middle of the night and turned off my phone. Naively going back to sleep and thinking maybe I'd revisit the idea of Butch and his buddies after I finished The Enchanter Series in a few years.

I knew Butch was in the 80's just doing his thing towing cars, watching Knight Rider, and jamming to Creedence Clearwater Revival, and I wasn't sure if a contemporary romance was a direction I wanted to go yet. If ever.

But, buuuut, Butch Casady had other plans. And he's quite the persistently stubborn man. I mean, when he knows what he wants, he goes after it. It's kind of hot, so I can't really fault the guy. But seriously, he would not leave me be!

As soon as I had finished Thatcher and Rosalie's story in Dark Succession - as in, a day later - I started writing a few chapters of Butch. My thought being if I started his story, he'd maybe back off a little. Take a breather from his incessant sexy and gravelly, deep-voice talkin'.

Boy, was I wrong.

Two chapters turned into ten, which turned into 20, which turned into the whole gosh darn book! It took me less than a month for Butch's tale to be told from start to finish and, truth be told, I loved every minute of being his storyteller!

And the music I listened to on my earbuds as I wrote to shut out the world I was in and immerse myself in the world *he* was in was one of the best parts!

There's something about music that enhances an experience, yeah?

I hope you enjoy your visit to Eddington, Ohio where the boys are tough, the grandma's are tougher, and the Quick Mart is open all night long!

PS: If someone could please tell Butch's best bud, Wren, that I need a breather before I start another story, that would be super great. For such a quiet guy, Wren certainly likes to chat with me!

Those Eddington boys are a handful!

PPS: I can't help but think you will have dreams of Butch after reading this book, as well! Maybe we should start a club - Butch's Dream Girls?

BUTCH PLAYLIST

Total Eclipse of the Heart - Bonnie Tyler
Holding Out for a Hero - Bonnie Tyler
Every Little Thing She Does is Magic - The Police
You Shook Me All Night Long - AC/DC
Drive - The Cars
I Want to Know What Love Is - Foreigner
Crazy for you - Madonna

ONE
I KNEW I WANTED HER

Eddington, Ohio

April, 1985

Wiping the grease off my hands, I gently close the hood of the Firebird.

Looking down at the smooth, clean lines of the snorkel scoops, I remember the first time I laid eyes on the bombshell. As soon as I saw her, all smashed up in her blazing glory, I knew I wanted her.

The original owner, an asshole with a dickhead complex, ran right off the road, down an embankment, and straight into an old oak tree after getting shitfaced at KJ's. When I pulled the poor girl out of the sticks and mud, her entire front was crunched in. But her sides and back? As sleek and pretty as the day is long. Sure, she had a few scratches here and there, but nothing that couldn't be buffed out. And even though she wasn't mine, I handled her with kid gloves that night giving her the respect she deserved.

1

I towed her to Wren's shop that night, and the asshole dickhead was thrown in the county slammer to sleep off his Fuzzy Fuckin' Navels. I don't know when it happened, but our sleepy little town's only bar had become a popular haunt on the weekends for all the big city pussies from Calverton to enjoy a "podunk honky tonk" experience. Whatever the fuck that was.

When momma's boy woke up the next morning with a raging headache from his overconsumption of sissy drinks and a bill for service, not to mention a hefty fine for driving around our quaint town under the influence, he called his daddy long distance. He promptly informed the brat he was no longer bailing his scrawny ass out after a night of bad decisions.

Being the nice fucking guy I am, I offered to buy the car off of him. For the exact amount he owed the city of Eddington for services rendered. I recognized the look of desperation and I pounced.

Pretty boy with soft hands had never had to work a day in his life. He certainly had never been forced to figure out his own problems before. And with a credit card that no longer had the unlimited funds he was accustomed to, he happily took the offer and skipped out of town with nothing but the preppy clothes on his back.

I've been babying the 1970 hotrod ever since. Completely rebuilt under the hood, I made her even better than before. And the crowning jewel, shining bright in the fluorescent light of my garage - a gilded gold Laughing Phoenix across the ebony formula hood. It took a little patience, but I finally found the mint condition hood at a scrap yard a few hours away. I was as giddy as a fucking kid at Christmas.

I haven't taken her out yet, what with snow and salt and all the sludge they spit at you when they're mixed together. So, she sits here in the garage next to my black Harley. But I'm looking forward to cruising back roads for hours this summer in both.

Hearing the double ring of the phone at the front desk and back here in the garage over the "Where the skies are so blue" part of "Sweet Home Alabama", I throw down my rag on the stool and wipe my hands across my blue jeans out of habit before turning the radio off and picking up the line.

"Butch."

"Hey Sunny. It's Joe."

My guys are real comedic geniuses. They use any damn chance they can get to call me by one of my unoriginal nick-names. Typically, they only use 'em over the CB radio, but they occasionally let it slip over the phone, too. And seeing as how my parents thought they were pretty fucking clever when they picked my name, I can't say I blame the boys for taking advantage of the annoyingly obvious stand-up material. I mean, how many people walk around with a name like Butch Casady?

Looking around the corner to the big lit up neon blue Chevy clock on the wall, I realize it's already almost five o'clock. I always lose track of time under my girl's hood. "What's up?"

"Listen, Mikey's not feeling well tonight and has been stuck on Jules all day. She's exhausted and -"

"Don't worry about it, man. I'm good here. You take care of yours."

There is a short pause and I swear I hear Joe sigh in relief. "Are you sure? I really appreciate it."

"Yeah. No problem. Let Julie get some rest. Make her a cup of hot tea or some shit."

Joe laughs into the phone and I hear little Mikey start to fuss up a storm in the background. "See ya later, man."

Hanging up the phone, I can't help the small jolt of jealousy I feel. Joe's one lucky son of a bitch. He's got a good woman and a new baby - a combination not so easy to come by around here.

It's no skin off my back to stay late. I have a good team of guys working for me. And if there is anything I've learned while being the boss, treating those who work for you with respect goes a long way. Not expecting your crew to do shit you wouldn't or don't want to do earns that same respect in return. My boys know I'll do anything for them. And I know for a fact they'll do the same for me.

I grab the remote and switch on the old tv stuffed in the corner by the desk. The local news is on and I turn up the volume so I can hear it in the back. *Butch's Towing* isn't really the kind of establishment that has people coming in the doors; unless they're picking up their wheels. And even then, that's a rare occurrence since I typically have to drop off whatever vehicle I've towed to the *Rollin' Right* mechanic and body shop down the road. I don't need a fancy waiting room like Wren's got over there.

My garage is pretty quiet this time of year. One guy in shop to man the phone and one on the road is the most we ever really need - at least until the flakes start dropping from the sky. That's when I do most of my business. Being the only towing service in the tri-county area, I get a lot of calls from Parksville, Hilford and occasionally Clarks Grove. And seeing as how I can charge extra for mileage and gas, I don't mind being the only hook and chain service around. Just coming out on the other side of busy season, we are all enjoying the slower pace.

Walking to the back of the shop, I decide I might as well make good use of my time since I'm here for a while. Grabbing the mop and bucket, I head to the slop sink to fill it up. It's been too long since the cement floor had a good scrub. Just because there's a mandatory layer of grease on practically everything you touch, doesn't mean it has to be filthy around here. Or so Granny tells me anytime she comes in.

Which reminds me, I still need to pick up a few cans of cat food for the old broad. I'll have to make a stop at the Quick Mart on my way home. I need beer anyway.

Throwing the bucket in the sink, I'm about to turn on the hot water when I hear the weather forecaster on the tube calling for more rain this week. Damn spring in Ohio. Guess I won't be getting my bike out anytime soon.

Two
Roses or Carnations?

Locking up for the night, I throw the garage keys in the pocket of my black leather jacket and hop into my reliable '75 pickup.

When the black beauty's rumbling and ready to go, I slam the door and grab the wheel, putting her in gear. The reflection from the *Butch's Towing* sign right above where we idle beams down onto the dark vinyl bench seat. Twisting my neck, I look up at the illuminated words. Just like I do every night before I drive away.

Granny Jean will be the first to tell you that I wasn't the brightest in school. Barely passed all the required courses. Struggled with math, struggled with reading, struggled with writing. Struggled with every fucking thing that makes up a school. Except for shop class. Taking a machine apart with my bare hands and putting it back together was something that I didn't need to think about. I just did it. And did it well.

Needless to say, college wasn't exactly on my radar. What the fuck would a kid with grease in his nails and permanently stained into his palms do in college anyway?

So instead of using the savings from my deceased parents

on college, I bought the old garage and three wrecker trucks from Dale instead. And changed the name from *Dale's Towing* to *Butch's Towing*. I clearly was not as good at the 'name game' as Mom and Dad.

Pulling out onto Main, I'm the only one on the road. Eddington is a quiet place at noon. It's a fucking ghost town at midnight.

Even though I only had one gig in Parksville tonight, I'm tired as hell. It was a long, busy winter and my body is still making up for it. But it looks like spring is finally going to stick around here, thank fuck.

A few miles down the road, I flip my turn signal on and pull into the Quick Mart. I don't know why Bobby keeps it open 24/7, but I'm grateful he does. Sometimes I swear he does it just for me. Well, not for *me* at all. But to get in Granny Jean's good graces. He's been chasing after her since I can remember. And I've been living with her since I was seven, so I can remember pretty God damn far back.

Pulling into the small parking lot, I have to squeeze my big truck around a piddly-ass yellow Pacer parked the wrong way right in front of the store. I don't recognize the car. And I would most definitely recognize that shitbox around town due to the fact that I'd probably have to tow the box of junk to Wren's all the fucking time.

Parking in an actual white-lined parking spot, I turn off the engine of my Chevy and immediately hear the thumping of the bass coming from the speakers of the little banana-colored Pacer. Shaking my head, I pass by on my way to the doors. The shithead in the driver's seat is too busy headbanging to some God-awful yelling about fighting to party to even notice anyone else around him. This jerk has some major little dick issues.

Pulling open the door, the familiar ding of the bell sounds and I look over to the young kid that typically mans the register Thursday nights. I turn up my chin in acknowledgement as I grab a metal shopping basket and make a b-line for the pet food aisle. There's nothing my grandmother loves more than me - except her cat. That spoiled brat showed up at her door one night a few years ago and has not been outside since. Living a high life of luxury, "Sam" is the king of the castle at her house. Only the best food, the best litter, the best toys. Jesus, if I wasn't so secure in my manhood, I'd be raving jealous of the furball.

Throwing a six-pack of Coors into the basket, I remember Granny asking me to pick up some Vaseline for Sam's hairballs. Shaking my head at the absurdity, I cut down the cleaning lane and turn down the one that has all the baby shit.

I stop at the sight of a short, pregnant girl on the tips of her toes attempting to reach a pack of diapers on the top shelf. I am certainly no expert on women and pregnancy, but she looks like there's a balloon in her shirt about to pop. Maybe it's the pink pants and the oversized pink top with a bow tied tight around her back that accentuates her belly.

"Need some help?" I ask, setting down my basket in front of her near empty cart. She jumps, and squeaks, crossing her hands in front of her in a knee-jerk reaction to being startled. Her brown curly hair is pulled back in a braid; little twists that have escaped the knot frame her face, and those huge blue eyes look up at me like a deer in headlights.

Raising my brows, I smirk at the small adorable face in front of me. I reach up and grab the bundle she was trying so hard to get, placing it in her cart next to a carton of milk. I push the twelve-pack of Old Milwaukee out of the way and put her loaf of white bread on top so it doesn't smash.

"Thank you," she whispers with her eyes down. I watch in interest as her round cheeks slowly flush in embarrassment. In what I am assuming is a fight-or-flight response, she pushes her shopping cart forward quickly in order to escape, ramming right into my basket.

The metal carrier filled to the brim with Frisky's knocks over and every one of the furball's food cans roll out in all directions. Well, shit.

Just as I am about to retrieve them, or leave 'em all over the damned floor and go home with my beer, the girl is apologizing and rushing to pick one up.

I grab her to stop her from unnecessarily taxing herself on my behalf, and as soon as my hand makes contact with her thin arm, she yanks it back nervously.

"Woah." Splaying my hands out in a peaceful gesture, I tell her quietly, "Hey, I'm sorry. No big deal. I can get 'em." I reach down to get one and I hear a clanking sound. Turning my head, I see she has placed one in the basket, too.

"Thanks," I say, smiling at her and accepting the help she obviously wants to provide.

Getting a timid and small smile in return, the two of us continue to collect the mini cans of fish flavored cat tuna scattered over the entirety of the aisle while *Total Eclipse of the Heart* echoes out of the ceiling speakers.

When we've gathered them all, I pick up the basket and

she begins to push her cart. We both quietly walk towards the front of the store. It's awkward as shit, and I don't know why, but I can't help but stare at her while she anxiously peeks at me out of the corner of her eyes.

Distractedly, I find myself wishing I could get close enough to count the number of freckles that dart across her cheeks and over that pert nose.

Yeah, Butch. Because that's not fucking creepy as hell.

Passing through the cereal aisle, I wait for her to pass and I cut across to grab a box of Wheaties. I notice out of the corner of my eye that she has slowed down and picked up a box of Lucky Charms, setting it down near the diapers.

"I don't care what the commercial says, there's nothing magically delicious about that shit."

She tries to hide the smirk on her face by putting her head down, but she's not quick enough. I catch a glimpse of what I am sure would be an amazing smile in its entirety.

A few steps farther and I veer off for a jar of creamy peanut butter while she's reaching for the chunky shit.

"Interesting choice," I mutter under my breath.

The sweetest sounding giggle erupts from her lips and a weird sensation pulls in my chest. Grabbing the edge of her cart, I pull it behind me the rest of the way to the cash register, pausing at the floral display on the end cap. I need to pick out Granny's weekly bouquet of fresh blooms. Not that she ever expects it, but I do it anyway. I love the surprise smile she gives me even though I've been delivering them once a week for goin' on a decade. And I know how much she enjoys showing off her flowers on the kitchen table during card night with the church ladies.

"Roses or carnations?" I ask the girl standing behind the handle of the cart. At first, she appears shocked that I've spoken to her again, but then, she pulls her plump lower lip in her teeth. Deep in thought.

"Carnations." Her voice, still quiet as hell, is the loudest it's been in all of our short conversations.

I raise my eyebrow. "Roses are the darlin' of flowers, sweetheart."

Again, that smirk on those lips. "Yes, but carnations are survivors. They stay brighter and live longer."

"Hm," I grunt, putting the red carnations in my basket. "Can't argue with that."

When we get to the sales counter, I reach around her to lift up the box of beers for her. The smell that hits my nose from her hair, or her body, or wherever the hell it's coming from, makes me reel back. The girl smells like candy. Like a perfectly wrapped piece of butterscotch. Or caramel. Maybe vanilla - I don't fucking know. All I know is that a girl that looks like that, and walks around smelling like that, tends to taste like that, too.

Chucking the beer on the belt with a little more effort than necessary, I try to get a grip on my creepy ass thoughts.

"Thanks again," her sweet voice lilts behind me and I smile back to her as I lift up her milk, cereal, peanut butter and bread. The diapers are the last thing to go up and just as I'm about to inquire where she's from, not sure why I even care, the repetitive honking of a horn draws all of our attention outside.

Right out the double glass door, is the asshole still sitting in the lemon Pacer. Only now instead of flipping his mullet in beat to his music, he's irritatingly honking and yelling at us.

"What the hell?" I ask the kid at the cash box. Shrugging his scrawny royal blue Quick Mart vested shoulders, he looks as confused as I am.

"Can I get a pack of Marlboro's, too, please?" The musical voice belonging to my mystery shopping partner chimes in. "And, can you go a bit quicker?" Looking around me at the banana mobile practically jumping off the concrete from the booming bass, she urges, "Please?"

Nodding his head, the kid finishes ringing up her items and reaches behind him for the cigarettes. Bagging her handful of groceries as fast as he can, all while nervously keeping an eye on the bum in the car outside, he leans over to read her total from the register screen. "That will be $17.31, ma'am."

"Oh," the word causes a crack in her voice. "Um, maybe -" At this point she looks ready to burst into tears. And damn it all to hell, nothing gets to me like a woman crying. Pulling out a few wrinkled bills from her pocket, I see a worn ten and a five. "Can you just take the cereal off the order?"

The persistent beeping continues, only now the asshat's got his head out the window and he's yelling shit that I can't make out through the door. I look from him to her, connecting the dots. And I shake my head. What a fucking shame.

Following orders, the kid's reaching over to take her box of marshmallow cereal from the brown paper bag, I wave his hand away. "I got it," taking a twenty from my wallet and tossing it on the belt. Receiving another quivery, near-whispered, "Thank you," before she walks around me.

I watch her hurriedly trying to lift the paper bags into her arms, all while the stand-up guy in his loser cruiser just glares at her like he's miffed she's taking so long.

"Son of a bitch," I say between my teeth. Putting down my basket on the belt, I toss down another twenty and motion to the poor kid just trying to do his job, waiting to get back to his uneventful night watching MTV behind the counter. "Go ahead and ring me up. I'll be right back, buddy." No matter how much I want to tell that guy out there with his stupid hair and even mores stupid music to fuck off, Granny taught me better.

Walking up to her struggling little form trying to figure out how to hold the bags around her stomach, I grab the groceries from her arms and open the door, propping it with my worn cowboy boot.

She doesn't move. Those baby blues staring intently down at the cheap linoleum tile, timidly twisting and squeezing her fingers together in front of her.

"We gonna stand here all night, sweetheart?" Motioning out the door with my chin, "Not that I mind, but your pal's gettin' pissy."

Getting her tiny ass in gear, she squeezes between me, her groceries, and the frame of the door and I swear I have to clench my eyes closed at the closeness of her smell. God damn.

Following her to the car with the muffled shit tunes, she opens the passenger door and is immediately assaulted with a puff of stale cigarette smoke and a, "Finally! What took so long?"

So immersed in himself, he doesn't even notice me standing off to the side of his car holding his girl's fucking groceries. And when I hear her apologize to him, I grip the bottom of the bags tight to keep myself from flipping the teeny-weeny punk over in his teeny-weeny car.

She pulls the first bag from my arms without even a glance my way and bends down to push it behind the passenger seat, quickly turning around for the second bag. As she tugs it from my grip, she spots the red carnations sitting on top of the box of beer and those blue doe eyes move up to me in confusion. "I think you can use a little strength, tonight darlin'. Granny will understand."

Still confused, tears fill up her eyes. Fuckin' hell, here we go again.

"Let's goooooo!" Mini dick calls out again.

Just like that, she's tucking her small body and oversized belly into the passenger seat and he's peeling away, barely stopping to check for incoming traffic before squealing out onto Main Street and off to wherever the hell they're going.

And I'm standing here scratching my head wondering what just happened.

THREE
WHY IS THIS HARD?

Eddington, Ohio

November, 1987

One of these days I'm going to figure out what makes people lose the ability to drive the first snowfall of the season.

We live in Ohio. The skies drop white flakes for nearly six months.

Every goddamn year.

Why is this hard?

I back up my red wrecker truck to one of the closed roll-up doors, hopping out and stretching my back. I've been on the road since three in the morning. Considering it's quarter till seven and I haven't eaten all day, I'm in a shit mood. And looking around, there's only one other tower in the lot. Meaning one of my guys is still out hooking up cars.

Walking around the other truck and entering through the one open roller into the garage, KITT's computerized voice broadcasts from the tv up front. I wonder whose ass

Hasselhoff'll kick tonight.

My stomach is growling like a rabid dog. But first thing's first, I've got to make a call. Picking up the phone in the back, I dial the number I know by heart. I get three rings and then a, "Yeah?"

"Gran, how's it goin'? Everything okay there? The weather's shit - you need anything?"

"Butch Casady, don't go calling me up and cursing to me over the phone. You know I don't like that talk in person. I damn sure don't like it over the phone!"

Never one to argue with Granny Jean, I chuckle. The apple didn't fall far from the family tree when it comes to personality. "You're good."

"Yeah, I'm good. Don't worry about me. Worry about you and make sure you get home in one piece. You can't keep working these hours. It's too much."

"I think things are settling down. I'll be home in a bit."

I hear her humph into the phone. "I'm serious, Butch. You need to let go a bit and hire a few more guys. You're working yourself ragged. And how are you ever going to give me grandbabies if you're married to your garage?"

Sighing in defeat, I say, "Alrighty. Good talk, Gran. I'll see you later, yeah?"

She hangs up just as Joe walks out from the bathroom, drying his hands off on his pants. Always a skinny guy, his grey "Butch's Towing" shirt practically hangs off his body.

He throws his chin out in greeting. "Hey Sunny. Just heading out to a call out on 77. Three-way collision. Barry's going head out that way once he drops his load off to Wren."

I shake my head in response. Just gotta remind myself that

even though it's hard, back-breaking work, my house is paid off, my cars belong only to me and my business is booming.

"You need me to come along?"

Joes already halfway in his truck, the door propped open with Barry's voice sounding over the CB radio. "Nah. We'll be fine. Sounds like one of the cars is still drivable. Just a bunch of teens goin' too fast."

"Sounds good." I head towards the old Kenmore fridge against the back wall. I'm pretty sure I've still got a box of New Hunan beef and broccoli in there from the other night.

Just about to yank his door closed, Joe calls out, "Hey, Mikey's birthday is Saturday. Jules is really hoping you'll make it out. Her friend's going to be there!"

Shit. I forgot all about it. Pulling the handle of the fridge, I grab the paper carton and sniff what's inside. "Yeah, Kelly, right?"

Laughing, Joe revs up his engine and calls out, "Her name's Kayla."

Not bothering to look back at what I'm sure is an annoying smile on Joe's thin face, I tell him, "Maybe," and raise my hand up in a quick 'good bye and fuck off' wave before I stab some cold beef with the plastic fork I left in the box. I walk towards the tv to sit in the one decent chair in the place.

Why the hell did I agree to let his wife play this Matchmaker shit? As if the few women in my life aren't enough of a headache already. Maybe it's because I grew up letting my dick do the talking, but I haven't made the best choices when it comes to broads. And I've been playing the same game with Tina for so long I've grown tired and weary of the idea of trying to date again. That shit's exhausting.

I thank God every day that the one time I actually listened to Granny Jean was when she told me not to marry her. Well, actually, she said, "Butch, Tina will never be anything more than a girl. You need a woman. And we'll both be miserable the rest of our lives with her in it."

At least with Gemma, we were both in it for the same thing. Or at least, that's what it was in the beginning. I'd head to KJ's for a few beers, and if Gemma was tending the bar, and we were both in the mood, I'd follow her up to her place above the bar after her shift. No strings, no attachments, no expectations. Nothing Granny would be proud of, but it scratched the itch, if you catch my drift. And seeing as how my buddy Kurt owned the fine establishment in which she was employed, the both of us steer clear of dramatics.

Chomping on a huge piece of broccoli, I decide not to worry about Saturday until Saturday. Turning up the volume, I mindlessly watch Knight Rider until I hear the sound of an engine outside and I look down to see the leftover Chinese is gone.

Standing up, I stretch and my back pops in about a hundred places. I squint up at my silver wristwatch above my head. I hate jewelry of any type, but I can't stand not knowing the time. Plus Granny gave it to me the year I bought the garage. It's one of the only things of value my Grandfather ever owned. Granny said she'd been saving for the right time to give it to me, and I've worn the Rolex everyday ever since. And right now, it reads 8:17. Shit, I've been out of it for over an hour. I need to go home and crash.

I look over my shoulder as Barry walks in the back door, looking as beat as I feel. "Let's call it a night, bud. If anyone needs me, they can reach me at home."

Turning around, he heads straight back out the door, "I'm not gonna argue. See ya tomorrow boss."

Flipping the switch on the tv, I turn the lights off in the front of the building and toss my empty food carton into the trash can by the desk. Walking around to make sure the front door is locked, the phone rings.

Sighing, I have a feeling this call's going to ruin my plans. I pick up the dirty cream-colored receiver. "Butch."

"It's Jax." Getting a call from the police chief is never good. But getting a call from the police chief during the first snowstorm of winter? Bad news. "I've got a girl here broke down on 18. My scanner's going crazy, Judy's panicked at the station, and I have just enough time to call you and make sure she's covered. She's got a kid with her and the weather's gettin' pretty bad."

My buddy, Jax. Ever the do-gooder. Grew up alongside me, Kurt, and Wren. We always knew he'd wind up serving and protecting for a living. It's what he's best at. "Alright. I'll radio out to Joe and -"

"I'd rather it be you, Butch. I'm already feeling shit for having to leave her out here in this mess. I need to know she's safe. Nothin' against Joe, but I'm not going to know that unless I know it's you that's coming."

I close my eyes and sigh. "Roger that. I'm heading out now."

Well, shit. There goes my night. Not only am I going to chain up another car, but I'm going to be responsible for a broad and her kid until I can get her to Wren's. And he's not open until tomorrow morning, which means I'm going to have to figure out what the fuck to do with them until he is. It's not like I can leave her and her kid in the back lot until he can get to them like I do cars.

Picking the receiver back up, I dial the seven-digit number written on the tab under the dial next to a poorly scribbled out name in pencil. The phone rings five times before his machine picks up. "It's Wren. You know what to do," followed by a drawn-out high-pitched beep. "I've got a dead car on 18 I'm picking up now. There's a situation with the driver. I need you to call me."

Not that it's Wren's problem either, but he at least has a decent waiting room with vending machines for them to hang out in as the storm passes and her car is fixed.

Grabbing my leather jacket, I throw it on and walk back out to my truck, turning off lights and locking up as I go.

Four
It's You

Dragging down the highway, it's a white-out all around me as I search for the broke down car.

Damn it, I wish I was in my warm bed.

Passing by what appears to be a small, gold car pulled off to the side of the lane, I make out the shape of someone sitting in the driver's seat through the dark fogged up windows.

Turning on the blinkers, I pull over onto the berm, straighten out the wheels, and reverse the wrecker until my back bumper is at the front of the car.

I flip on the hazards, tighten my knit hat, and open the door. Hopping out, I'm about to close the door behind me when a nasty wind whips through the air and almost pulls the heavy door out of my hands. "Shit!" I climb right back in but keep my feet on the running boards as I reach behind the seat to grab the emergency red checkered blanket I have stored back there for situations just like this. I switch on the heat to the high setting, also making sure all the vents are open and blowing hard.

Getting out again, I close the door behind me, tucking the blanket in the crook of my arm and pulling on my gloves.

Walking up to the car, the first thing I notice is the darkness. No lights and no engine typically mean alternator problems. The driver's side door opens and a small woman steps out. Her curly hair blows all over the damn place. She has no coat, no gloves, but crosses her arms in front of her in defense of the raging weather happening around her.

"Are you Butch?" She yells out over the wind, closing her door.

"Yep," I bellow back. "You got a kid in there, right?"

She nods her head, cupping her hands to look in the back side window into the car with concern.

"Here," I reach out, giving her the plaid fleece. "Why don't you two get in the truck where it's warm while I work out here?" I can barely make out her face, but the snow is collecting on her long eyelashes and I can only imagine she's cold as hell sitting out here and now standing in it.

"Thank you!" She says as she grabs the blanket and quickly opens the door and reclines the front seat forward, most of her body disappearing in the car. When she emerges, she has a small bundle all wrapped up in the blanket. She walks by me to head towards the truck and the scent of cookies briefly fills my nose. The kid must have a snack under all those layers.

I wait until they are both safe inside my truck before I start lowering the crane so that I can hook onto the axle of the tiny car being covered in snow. When I see the Pacer car badge on the bottom of the door, I shake my head. No woman and child have any business being out in this shit in *this* shit car.

I double check my chains and jog towards the truck, the snow collecting like crazy all around. The storm has gotten wicked over the past few hours.

Opening the door, I jump up into the truck, "All set out there. How's everyone doin' in here?" I ask, pulling the door against the wind and shutting it roughly.

As soon as I'm shut in the cab with my passengers, I identify the cookie smell. And it isn't Tollhouse, that's for damn sure. Staring at those baby blues, it all comes together. The smell, the car, the eyes I'm staring into.

My mouth drops open. "It's you."

And just like that those eyes go from warm to confused in a matter of seconds. Realizing I'm wearing my cap and covered in snow, I reach up and remove the hat. Running my fingers through my hair. It's gotten longer than I normally let it, but I thought I'd see what it was like. Honestly, I don't care either way, I guess I was just feeling a little lazy.

"You, ah, you probably don't remember me. But I think we met a few years back?" I look at the little girl sound asleep on her lap, her little head the only thing visible under the plaid. A miniature replica of the woman holding her, covered in pink from her toes up to the bow on top of her head, my brain does the math and it adds up. It was about 2 years ago since we first met. I notice the petite hands wrapped around the girl tighten and I lift my eyes to a now weary face. It is a slight movement, barely perceptible, but I saw it when she moved closer to the door - and farther away from me.

Drawing my brows in, I twist up the volume of the CB, tune in to channel 19, and pick up the microphone to radio in to Jax. "Sundance here, over."

Looking down between us, I see there's two diapers sitting on the seat. I don't remember seeing her grab a purse.

I hear the static and the familiar voice. "You got her?" He

asks.

"10-4, buddy."

Replacing the microphone into the cradle, I look over and smile at the woman. Her curly hair is wet from the snow she stood in when I first arrived and her cheeks are pink. She's wearing an oversized cream knit sweater and black pants. Her shoes look like loafers. Whatever the fuck they are, they're not snow boots. And the kid isn't in a coat. Neither one of them are prepared to be out in this weather.

"I appreciate this," she mutters under her breath, her eyes staring straight out the windshield.

Shit. Maybe I'm wrong? Maybe it's not her. Feeling like a first-class idiot, I place the truck in gear and check behind me for oncoming traffic before I pull out onto the empty highway.

It's quiet in the cab, the only sound the air blowing full blast from the vents. Every time I breathe in, I inhale that same sweet candy smell from all those years ago, and I swear it's the same woman that's invaded my thoughts entirely too much since that middle of the night encounter.

Not that it matters. We spoke for, what? Maybe fifteen minutes? And I wouldn't exactly call it "speaking". If I recall, it was more like me speaking and her staring down at her damned feet until I paid her bill and she drove away with that schmuck stick. Why do I even care? I'm just tired, I tell myself. I need this night to be over, the snow to stop, and a warm meal in my stomach.

Slowly turning onto the open median, I check both ways before carefully pulling out and heading back towards town.

"I remember you." She says quietly and I look over to her,

my brows raised. But she doesn't turn her head. "The Quick Mart, right?"

"Ah - yeah. Yep."

"Sundance?" She asks, turning her pretty face back to me with her eyebrow cocked.

"It's a nickname that I could never get rid of. No matter how hard I tried," I answer.

"Is your last name Cassidy?"

Pursing my lips out, I nod my head. "Spelled different though."

And that is it. That is all we say the rest of the way back to town.

But that doesn't stop my mind from trying to figure out what I am going to do with these two once we make it back to the garage. Once we pass the "Welcome to Eddington" sign, I have only come up with two viable options.

Pulling under my neon sign, I park the truck but leave it running, turning to my newly acquired passenger. "Here's the deal, darlin'. It's the middle of the night. Wren's not in his shop until tomorrow morning, and the snow's coming down hard and fast. If we stay here in the garage, we'll be snowed in for the night. Now, that's not a big issue, but it's not exactly warm in there and it's definitely not kid-friend-ly." I jerk my chin towards the little girl still knocked out. "There's no place else open right now. We can either stay here for the night, or you can come back to my place to wait out the storm. Hopefully we'll be able to get you out, into Rollin' Right, and on your way to wherever you were goin' at first light, either way."

That wariness shadows her face again and her bottom lip

gets sucked in her teeth as she contemplates our dilemma. Jesus, those lips.

Roughly wiping my eyes, I take a deep breath before I rest my arms across the top of the steering wheel and stare ahead at my brick building to give her a moment to figure it all out in her pretty little head. But, when she says nothing for what seems like forever, I look back over.

"Sweetheart, I'm not tryin' to be pushy, but we don't exactly have all the time in the world here. A few more minutes sittin' still, and here's where we'll sit for the remainder of the evening."

Looking hesitantly from the white painted brick in front of us and back to me, she says, "We'll go to your house." Pulling her daughter closer and tighter onto her lap, she goes back to staring out the truck window.

"Done." I put my black winter cap back on and say, "I've gotta go clean up my personal truck and get her warmed up for us. Probably gonna need to shovel her out, too. You girls sit tight, yeah?"

Nodding in acknowledgment, I give her an easy smile and get out as fast as I can so as not to wake up the sleeping one with the blast of cold air.

Trudging through the accumulating white shit, I shake my head. Never in a million years would I have guessed that I'd ever see her again. I mean, sure, she passed through my mind every once in a while, (for whatever the hell reason, I don't know). But to have her sitting in my cab right now? It's a crazy damn world, that's for sure.

Once the Chevy's cleaned off and warming up, I tromp back through the snow, already significantly higher than when I started.

Getting closer to the truck, I see her watching me through the window. Opening the door, I tell her, "You're sittin' pretty high and the snow's deep. Why don't you pass her over to me before you hop down and I'll carry her to the Chevy?"

She looks at me like I'm crazy. "I'll carry her. I'll be fine."

Sighing, I shake my head. "Sweetheart, you're in summer shoes and no coat." She looks down at her feet, like she's surprised I noticed her shoes. "Now, if you fall out there, I'll catch you. But if you fall while carrying her? When I could have both of you safely in my grip? I'd never forgive myself."

Mistrust written all over her face, I shake my head in disappointment. I know she doesn't know me from Adam, but the fact that she doubts my intentions bothers me more than it should.

She says to me quietly, "Please, be careful with her."

"I swear it," I say, picking up the bundled little one on her lap.

She's light and fragile, and when I place her against my chest, making sure the blanket's tucked all around her, the tiny head buries in tight right under my neck. I swear I feel a sigh of contentment easing out from her small body. This kid's out like a light. Carefully wrapping my arm tight around the back of her legs, her little butt resting on top of my arm, I look up to the woman wearily regarding me. "Do me a favor, switch off the lights and pull the keys."

Reaching over the seat, she does what I ask and turns to hand me the keys. Once I've placed them in my jeans pocket, I reach up to her to help her down. Grabbing my hand, I assist her out of the truck, pulling her out of the way so that I can close the door.

With her elbow firmly in my left hand, and her daughter firmly in my right, we make our way back through the snow to the running vehicle.

"Try to step in the foot tracks I've already made," I tell her, every step I take feels like I'm carrying a box of irreplaceable China.

Her short legs have to hop to do so, but she hits every one and a small smile pulls up my lips.

Once we're in the truck and she's got her kid back in her arms, out of the corner of my eye, I see her lay her head back and sigh, exhaustion taking over her pretty face.

"House is only 10 minutes away."

She nods, twisting her neck so she's staring back out the window at the moving buildings we pass.

Trying to remember the last time I did the dishes and vacuumed, I think about the bathroom and hope to God I flushed before I left.

"Help yourself to the radio," I offer, attempting to break the silence. She looks to me, to the radio, and then back out the window.

I give her a few minutes and try again, "I figure, since we're going to be spending the night together, I should at least know your name."

Giving me an incredulous side eye, she scoffs, "We are *not* spending the night together."

Well, that earned me a response. Not exactly the sweet doe eyes and whispered words, but it's something.

Smirking at her purposeful misunderstanding of what I

was trying to say, I probably don't help matters when I tell her, "Darlin'. That's not what I meant and you know it. But, if it's your way of expressin' interest, just so we're clear, I wouldn't kick you out of my bed."

"You're ridiculous," she says incredulously.

I can't help myself when I wink at her. Waiting a few seconds, I prod, "Name?"

Her voice is short and curt, "Francine."

"Hm." I grunt, turning onto my road.

"Hm, what?" She questions, sounding a tad bit pissy.

"*Hm*, I'm not surprised that your name is somethin' fancy like Francine." I answer as I slowly turn in my driveway, clicking off my lights to keep them from shining into the house right next to mine. I live in an older neighborhood and the houses were built pretty close together but with nice sized lots in the front and back. Mine is one of the biggest ones on the street, though the one next to mine is the same layout, just on a much smaller scale.

The Chevy glides smoothly over the piled-up flakes. I need to remember to thank Wren for hooking me up with these snow tires.

"It's not fancy," she huffs. "It's a family name. My grand-mother's name, actually."

Parking the truck, I glance over to her and notice her sit up higher in the seat, her pert nose going a bit further up in the air. I chuckle. "It's fancy." And before she has a chance to retort, I hop out, slam my door, pocket the keys, and walk around to her side. She pushes her door open and kicks her leg around the seat to get out.

"Woah." I say, putting my hand on her thigh to keep her

moving. Her eyes dart from my hand to my face. "Same deal as before, darlin'. But, this time, you're not getting out and walking in this. The sky's been at it all day, and I had the garage lot shoveled this afternoon so it wasn't as bad."

My hand rests on the back of the child between us. "I'll take her in and get her settled on the couch, and then I'll come back out for you."

I hear a heavy huff of breath, but there's no argument. She smoothly transfers the wrapped-up kid to me, miraculously still conked out, and slides her leg back in the cab before I close the door.

Walking up the drive and around the house to the back, I prop open the storm door with my foot and unlock the house. Stomping my feet off on the threshold, I enter through the kitchen and into the family room. Slowly, I place the bundle of pink on my leather couch. Grabbing another blanket, I make sure she's tucked in good and tight before passing by the old rocking chair and switching on the lamp sitting on the end table between the furniture pieces.

Heading towards the kitchen, I hesitate and turn around, going back to the rocking chair. Untying the cushions from the wood spindles in the back, I lay the flat pillows down in front of the couch in case the little one rolls over while we're outside.

On my way back out, I flip the switch on the kitchen. Hesitant to wake up the kid when we first came in.

The truck door is open by the time I get back to it, and Francine steps out onto the running board. I don't say anything before I wrap my arms around the back of her legs and pull her up and off.

Francine's got one arm around my neck, which I don't mind at all, and I kick the door closed and make the trip back to the house. The curtains moving in the dark window next door leaves me grinning, knowing full well how snoopy the neighbor lady is.

Once we're inside, I set Francine down on her feet. Predicting exactly what she's about to ask. I assure her, "She's in the family room on the couch." Nodding my head towards the room. "I don't know what you feed her, but the kid sleeps like a champ."

Taking a few steps into the kitchen, Francine wraps her arms around her middle. Feeling like a dolt, I realize she's probably cold. I tend to keep the heat on low unless I'm expecting Granny Jean. I disappear into the dark dining room to adjust the thermostat, hearing the familiar sound of it kicking on as I walk back into the kitchen.

"It should warm up pretty quick." I tell her as I shove my hands in my pockets, finding her looking around the room.

It's nothing spectacular, but it's a decent sized kitchen with wallpapered walls, solid oak cabinets and built-in oak shelves along the end panels. It was all here when I bought it about a year ago, and I'm not one to fix something' if it ain't broke, so it's how it stayed. She picks up one of the framed pictures on the corner shelf, tucked near the doorway to the formal dining room, and I use her distraction to turn around real quick to check the sink behind me. Thankfully, other than my coffee mug, spoon and a beer can, it's somewhat clean.

I watch as she moves to the round oak kitchen table pushed towards the wall in front of the big picture window.

The window overlooks my backyard. It's a view I love to enjoy in the early mornings before work. Those round blue eyes slide to mine as her hands slide across the surface. "Do you live here alone?"

"Yep."

She looks at me like she doesn't believe me. "I've never met a guy with flowers on his walls and framed pictures in his kitchen."

While the little blue flowered wallpaper isn't exactly my thing, I don't think there's anything wrong with it. It's kind of grown on me, actually. And as far as the pictures, they were a housewarming gift. A picture of me with mom and dad before the car crash and one of me and Granny in front of the garage; Wren took it for us the day I bought it.

"Yeah, well." Not sure what to say, I rock on my feet, "Would you like some coffee?"

"That would be great, thanks." She says, walking into the family room.

I dump out the pot and rinse it under hot water before filling it back up. I pour it into the reservoir and lean over to the side cabinet, pulling out the canister of coffee and a new filter. Looking out the little window above the sink, I can see the thick flakes falling from the sky. We got here just in time. It wasn't the best weather before, but now it's a blizzard.

After the coffee maker's all set up and the water's brewing, I hang up my coat and hat in the hall closet at the front of the house before I follow Francine into the comfortable blue carpeted room off the kitchen. Even with the plain white walls and almost empty wall-to-wall bookshelf, the room is still the homiest spot in the house. The brown leather couch sits between two smaller windows that look right out into the house next door's windows. I usually keep the shades drawn, but the big window in the back keeps the room bright during the day. A twin to the window in the kitchen, except this one has a seat built-in.

Francine is crouched on the cushions I put on the floor earlier, sweetly brushing the little ringlets of hair off of her daughter's face.

"Make yourself at home." Picking up the remote from the side table, I place it on the end of the couch. "Feel free to recline out on the La-z-boy if you'd like," referring to the brown corduroy chair in the corner by the window. "I'm going to head upstairs and take a shower."

"Okay," she says softly and I'm rewarded with a small smile. God damn. Two years later and my body still reacts to every little thing she does. And I don't even fucking know her.

Nearly out in the hall, I remember my manners. Turning back towards her, I tap the wood trim of the doorway. "Oh, yeah. There's a bathroom right here," I point to the small bathroom to the left on the other side of the hall. Tucked between the family room and the kitchen, the only things in there are a toilet, sink, and small window overlooking the brick patio that sits just outside the back door. "And the coffee should be done soon. There's milk in the fridge and sugar on the cabinet. I don't tag you as the black coffee type."

Tapping the trim one more time, I cut to the right and through the dark living room toward the steps. The living room is what made me love the house. I'd have bought it regardless considering its location, but the hardwood floors and original brick fireplace, with the painted white fancy wood trim bows and the matching mantle spanning across the top, made the house perfect. The family room is long and narrow with a plush, comfortable carpet. But this room was built around the hearth. Therefore, I have one couch sitting right across from it and another along the interior wall. I picked cream colored furniture for the space, simple but clean. I'm no interior decorator, and white's pretty easy to match. So, other than the wallpaper in the kitchen, the rest of the house has white walls.

An old colonial, with the staircase centered and facing the front door, it's definitely more space than I need. Four living spaces downstairs, three bedrooms upstairs, two bathrooms, and full basement; the house was built for a family.

Reaching the top of the steps, I start to pull the shirt off my head and am overwhelmed by Francine's candy smell. Fuck. Must have been from when I picked her up and carried her in.

Balling the plain white shirt up and raising it to my nose so that I can breathe it in in all of its entirety, I realize what I'm doing and toss it on the floor.

Maybe a cold shower is what I need.

Five

Anytime Darlin'

I make the shower quick. And frigid.

Wrapping a towel around my waist, I head into my room and put on clean jeans. I stop to make my bed, or at least pull the sheet and quilt back over the mattress.

Coming down the steps, everything on the first floor is quiet and I don't hear the tv, leaving me to wonder what Francine's been up to. For as tired as she seemed in the truck, I wouldn't be surprised if she was sound asleep just like the kid.

Walking back through the dark living room and into the hallway, I quiet my steps as I round the corner of the family room and find Francine curled up on the window seat, her legs folded in front of her, a mug of coffee in her hand. She must have turned off the lamp and is sitting in the dark, her head leaning against the wall as she watches the snowflakes through the large window. Just like I like to do.

Lost in her profile, I make out her curly brown hair falling just past her shoulders. Hell, I can make out the individual spikes of her long lashes. And the deadly combination of her rounded cheeks and the natural pouty shape of her lips are enough to kill a man.

I have no idea how long I stand here staring at her before she turns my way. For a beat she just stares back before saying quietly, "You're staring, Butch."

"So are you, Franny." I say in way of answer, just as quietly.

There's an outline of a smile on her face before she's back to observing the flakes fall.

I walk over to the window seat and take a spot on the other side, crossing one leg in front of me in order to fit.

"It's beautiful." Francine murmurs.

My eyes absorb everything in front of them. Every movement and twitch. Every blink and breath. I could not give a goddamn about the snow. Having this woman in my home is nothing less than surreal. "Yes, it is." I say, not bothering to look away or hide my obvious fixation.

Her head turns and tilts slightly, "Are you always so forward with people you don't know?"

I practically laugh out loud at that question. Anyone who knows me knows I'm a man of few words with people I know. I don't typically say shit to people I don't.

But her? There's something different about her. And I felt it the moment I first met her. "I know you, Franny."

A tear slips down her cheek and my chest pulls. Instinctively, I reach out my hand and brush it away. I see her body tense, but she doesn't back away. The idea of leaving my hand cupped to her cheek is tempting, but I fight the urge and place it in my lap instead.

Resting her head back, she closes her eyes and whispers, "I'm so tired."

"You can take the bed upstairs."

Shaking her head back and forth, her eyes still closed, she

asks, "Have you ever felt lost? Like you've been wandering around trying to find your way in the dark. But no matter how hard you try, no matter what you do, you can never seem to find your way out?"

I don't say anything, feeling like she needs this moment to talk. And maybe not even to me, but just to say her thoughts out loud.

Angrily, she swipes her hands over her cheeks to wipe away more teardrops. "And then, then you finally find your way out, you *finally* break free from the darkness, only to find that even in the light of day, out in the open, you're still wandering? Still running from the darkness you escaped?"

My blood pressure is rising. I may not have any clue what exactly she's talking about, but I can put two and two together, and clearly, she's scared. My hands fisting, I ask, "What are you running from, Franny?"

A small grin curls those lips up, "My grandmother used to call me Franny. She's the only one that ever called me that."

Leaning forward, I cock a knee on the wood beneath us and rest my arm across it. Looking back at the little girl slumbering away on my couch, my eyes glide to Francine. "I need to know. And I need you to be honest with me right now. Are you two in danger?"

Taking a deep steadying breath, her eyes heavy, resting on the sleeping girl, she answers, "No. Yes. Maybe?" Her head falls back, and her eyes squeeze closed. "I don't know."

Well, that was as clear as mud. I help her out. "Here's what I know. And maybe you can fill in the blanks. Now, I'm no detective, but it doesn't take a degree to know that wherever you left from, you left in a hurry. You wound up stranded on the side of the road, partly because you're driving that piece of shit, but that's another subject. Neither one of you has a winter coat. No hat, no gloves, no boots. This storm has been all over the radio and news stations across the entirety of the Northwest region for a week. So, unless you emerged from under a rock this morning, I'm guessin' you knew about it, too. Meaning, you jumped quick. And when we left your car at the garage tonight, you didn't ask to grab a bag. No purse, no luggage. None of the shit you women usually carry on your person when you're *not* planning on being gone long. Add the fact that you've got a little one with you on top of that? Somethin' ain't right here.

"So, I'm going to ask again. What, or who, are you runnin' from, Franny?"

Taking a healthy gulp of coffee, she sighs. "When I first met Stephen, he was sweet. And funny. He had been the All-Star Football Captain at his high school in Hilford and was still riding that notoriety years later with no plans for his future. Add all that along with being from the other side of town? My parents disliked him. Immensely."

The sound of another man's name on her lips makes me clench my fists. And I have never been the jealous type. Unless, of course, you're talking about something that's mine.

"Naturally drawn to anything they dislike, I snuck around with him behind their backs. I was caught up in the glory of *finally* doing what I want. So caught up in the thrill of defiance, that I didn't see the obvious signs that were right in front of me."

"Don't get me wrong. He was good to me at first. And he actually *did* have money. But the warnings were always there. I just refused to acknowledge them - to question where he got his money or what he did at night. To do that would be to admit that my parents might have been right. And when I found out I was pregnant, I knew I couldn't go back home. I wouldn't be welcome back home without them turning it all about them. Richard and Whitney always cared more about their image than me. And even though they were wrong to judge Stephen just because he didn't live on the right side of town, because he wasn't going to Harvard, because his parents weren't members of the Country Club; they were actually right about him. Unfortunately, it was too late. We had run away. I had nothing. And I was pregnant. I needed him. And he knew it."

"But you stayed." I added, waiting for her to continue.

She looks at me defensively. "I had nothing. *We* had nothing. And I had been planning on leaving him all along. He was just ... my only way out." She laughs quietly, "I think he knew it. That's why he never let me out of his sight."

Rubbing her eyes, she continued, "Stephen had a large wad of cash when we first took off. I have no idea where he got it from. I can assume it was for or from drugs. Or theft even. But we had been living off of that. Until it ran out. Of course, he blamed that on me. Never mind the only money I ever spent was on food, things Lou Lou needed and to pay the lady in the apartment next door to babysit her for me while I worked. I knew I had screwed up. And I knew I had to fix it. For me and for Lucy Lou. So, I had been saving my tips from the diner, taking extra hours whenever I could, even picking up the graveyard shift. All of which were easy to do considering he couldn't keep a job longer than a week."

Setting her mug down next to her, she crosses her arms in front of her as if she's chilled. "When I woke up yesterday morning, we were out of diapers. I had worked all night and had asked him to pick up some during the day. Obviously, he didn't. Exhausted and frustrated, I had to ask him to use the car since he slept with the keys in his pocket." She laughs, "Afraid I was going to take off in the night, I guess."

"And did you?" I ask.

"No! I wouldn't have left until I knew I could properly take care of Lou Lou. I was close to it though. I'd been saving every penny I could and I was so close to making it out.

She rubs her eyes again. "I asked him for the keys. He was mad that I woke him up and threw them at me." Lifting her hair up off her head, I lean forward and can just make out the small cut in her neck thanks to the brightness of the snow outside.

She drops her hair down but I don't move back. "I was fatigued, having only gotten three hours of sleep. And I only had one hour to go to the store, feed the baby and make it back in time to drop her off to the sitters before I was expected back at the diner. I needed cash to pay for the diapers, and I was too afraid to ask him for anything else. In my rush, I was not as quiet as I should have been getting the coffee canister that held my measly savings out from where I kept it hidden in the kitchen. I had just shoved cash into my pocket when Lou Lou came from behind me and pulled on the mop handle in the closet I had opened, causing it, and the bucket it was in, to slam onto the floor. It was loud and she fell back with the mop, startling her and she started crying. I tried to comfort and soothe her. But he came storming in, angry at being woken up twice. He yelled at me to get her to stop crying. And I tried, standing up to rock her in my arms, but I knocked the can over and it wasn't sealed all the way. The money spilled out and..."

When she didn't finish, I leaned farther in, "Did he hurt you, Franny?"

"He pushed me around. And I was still holding Lou Lou when I fell. She hit her head on the table when we went down and I - I just lost it. I lost my mind at the sight. I picked up the nearest thing I could reach and threw it at him. A lamp, I think? I don't know if he was hurt because I ran out the door and jumped in the car. All I had on me was Lou Lou, the car keys and a twenty-dollar bill. I stopped a few towns away to get a few diapers and gas. And then I just drove. I drove to get as far away from him as I could."

I breathe in a steadying dose of air through my nose and concentrate on unclenching my fists. "Why don't you take the little sleeper over there upstairs and get some shut-eye, yeah? You two can take my bed. I've got a spare room, but the bed's not made up and I think we can both agree that neither of us is up for figurin' out a fitted sheet right now."

"What about you? Where will you sleep?" If I'm not mistaken, I hear a hint of panic in her voice. Fighting back the offense I feel at her discomfort towards me, I remind myself of everything she's been through in the last 24 hours.

"Those cushions are pretty damn comfy." I wink at her and lift my chin towards the bundle of blankets on the leather couch. "I think she can vouch for that."

Francine untangles her legs and reaches for her mug. But I put my hand over hers to stop her. "Nah. I got it, sweetheart."

Turning the small hand over so that her palm is cupping mine, she squeezes tightly. "Thank you, Butch."

I swear a fucking bolt of lightning went right up my arm the moment her hand held mine. And I'm pretty damn certain there's a crack in my voice when I tell her, "Anytime, darlin'.

Francine scoops up the little girl and gently walks out of the room. I listen as she goes upstairs, her light step releasing small squeaks from the aging hardwood. I track her footsteps above from the hallway, to the bed, to the bathroom, and back to the bed. I listen to the silence once she's safely tucked away under the comforter. And I think about everything she told me. And I make some serious decisions.

Six

Here

I crashed for a few hours, but had too much on my mind to sleep for long.

Around four I finally quit trying and decided to turn my brain off by putting my body to work. Starting with a shovel. I cleared the snow from the drive, sidewalk, and patio before I came in to see if my guests were awake.

No one was stirring the first or second time I poked my head into the kitchen between finishing up my own driveway and working on all the neighbor's.

And when I was finished with that, I brought wood in from the pile behind the shed so I could start a fire. The house is well-built, but old. And on cold snaps like this, the fireplace in the living room comes in handy to heat up the house faster than just the furnace alone.

Figuring the girls will be hungry when they do wake up, I whipped up some pancakes and eggs. And now, I'm sitting in front of the roaring fire with a fresh coffee in my hand, reading yesterday's newspaper.

The sound of stirring upstairs tells me the sleeping beauties have finally opened their eyes. After a few minutes, Francine rounds the corner holding the cutest damn little girl I have ever seen. Clearly, after all that sleep last night, she woke up bright eyed and happy. She's wearing a big smile and I look at those big blue eyes, just like her Mama's, take in the room around her before my own eyes land back on Franny. Standing in one of my white tees and a pair of my boxer shorts.

Damn, she looks good first thing wearing my shit.

"Good mornin'," I say to them both.

"Hi." She answers, "I hope it's okay I borrowed some of your stuff. I didn't have anything to wear to bed last night and my clothes were still wet from the snow."

"Darlin', you can wear my clothes every damn day."

Her round cheeks flush and she turns to the front window. The snow is coming down so thick you can barely see the elementary school right across the street. "Wow. It's still coming down pretty hard."

"Yep." Standing, I put the newspaper onto the couch and tuck my hand into my pocket. I move over to where they're standing and we watch the snow as I sip my coffee. "You hungry? There's fresh coffee and breakfast keeping warm in the oven."

Looking down at her daughter, Francine smiles. "We are starving. Thank you."

Walking into the kitchen, I grab plates from the cabinet and pull a handful of silverware from the drawer, setting them on the kitchen table. Following me in, she sits the little one in a chair and walks over to the counter. "Can I help?"

Sliding out the plate of pancakes and the bowl of scrambled eggs, I look at her and smile. "Nah. I got it." Turning around and dropping the food down on the middle of the table. "Take a seat and eat."

The phone on the wall rings and I take the chair in the corner, resting my foot across my leg, as I pick it up. "Yeah."

"I just got your message. My phone line was out. What's up?"

Leaning back against the chair, I observe the woman that has stuck with me from the first time I met her. "Hey. I've got a dead Pacer I need you to make priority."

Wren groans. "Shit. I hate those cars. Is it at the garage?"

Francine meticulously cuts the pancakes, patiently pulling back the little fingers that try to grab everything in front of her and she blows the eggs until they're cool, making perfect size bites.

"Uh, yeah, it's still on the lift. I'll have one of the boys get it down to you. I'm going to be takin' a few days off."

There was silence on the other end of the line before I hear, "The hell? You never take off work. What's going on Butch? Is everything okay?"

My eyes stay on Francine as she airplanes the spoon through the air and right into the wide-open mouth waiting for her next bite. "Yep. Just have some shit to sort.

Hanging up the phone behind me, I sit quietly and wait for her to start.

"Is there a hotel in town? Some place we could get a room for cheap?"

I reach across the table and pick up my coffee mug. "You're not stayin' in a hotel."

The fork is midair when she looks at me, "Well, we can't exactly just stay here!"

Taking a sip of coffee first, I say, "You're stayin' here."

She's shaking her head. "No. No, we can't. We can't stay here. I already owe you. There's going to be a mechanic bill that I don't know how I'm going to pay, we just - we can't." Her voice wavers, fighting off tears.

I let my leg slide off my knee. Leaning forward, resting my arms on my kneecaps. "Darlin', seein' as how you just admitted yourself you've got no way to pay for anything, you're going to stay here."

She lets out a deep sigh. "And then what, Butch?" She rubs her eyes. "We're not your problem."

"You're nobody's *problem*, Franny. And since you're the one in arrears, I'm the one that gets to decide how that favor is cleared. And we're going to start with you accepting that you're *not going anywhere*."

There's a knock on the door but I don't get up. I know exactly who's on the other side of that door.

Granny Jean lets herself in, closing the door behind her and stomping her boots on the floor mat. Just as I would have predicted, her skeptical face went from me, to Francine, and then the baby. At which any uncertainty she harbored regarding her late-night spying disappeared into a demeanor of pure sunshine.

"Well, who is this sweetie?" Faster than a woman her age should be able to move, she ditched her coat and boots and had the baby in her arms.

Francine looked questioningly from Granny to me and back to Granny. "Um, her name - her name is Lucy Lou."

"Well, hello Lucy Lou!" Granny coos, bouncing up and down with Lucy. "I'm Granny Jean. You and I are going to be the best of friends!"

Smiling at the sight of Granny, all 4'7" of her in her rainbow crochet sweater and tweed pants, completely in her element, having a child in her embrace, I introduce everyone. "Gran, this is Franny. Franny, this is my Granny Jean.

"Gran, Franny and Lou Lou are going to be staying here."

"For how long?" She asks, tapping Lucy's drooly chubby cheeks. Her voice may have an innocent chord, but I know better.

Franny looks at me in response to the question, and I answer without breaking her gaze. "A while."

"Well, I couldn't help but notice you came in empty handed last night. You two probably have errands to run for supplies. Go on ahead and get going." Granny says nonchalantly, walking into the warm living room with the baby.

"How does she know that?" Franny inquires, confusion written all over her face watching the tiny woman sashay out of the room with her daughter.

Chuckling, "Granny knows everything. She's the neighborhood busybody; and she lives right next door." My chin nods in the direction of the small white house to the right of mine. Franny turns in her seat to look out the window above the sink. "That's the house I grew up in. And when this one went on the market, it seemed like the most sensible solution. I can take care of her, and Granny can still have her independence."

Francine folds her small hands in her lap. "That's very kind of you, Butch. She's lucky to have you."

"Hm. So, are you going to go get cleaned up?"

Her brows raise, "Why? What for?"

"Sweetheart, Granny's no fool. She came here with a plan

47

in mind. Now go take a shower so we can head out and get all the shit we need before the day gets away from us. We still have a lot of setting up to do upstairs."

She stands up, but hesitates. "I'm sorry." Throwing her hands up in the air so they land in a slap at her sides. "I don't understand what's going on here."

I stand up too, pressing my hands down on the table as I lean towards her. "It's pretty simple, Franny. Lucy needs diapers, clothes, and whatever the hell else a kid needs. You need, well, everything I'm guessin'. So, we're going to go get it. Which we can't do, until you're dressed. So darlin', go."

Finally picking up that I'm not in the mood for more argument or discussion, she takes one last glance into the living room, whispers an, "okay," and heads upstairs.

Picking up the dishes on the table, I carry them to the sink and start cleaning up the kitchen.

Everything's wiped down and put away when Granny calls from the other room, "Butch! Bring in some Tupperware bowls and a few wooden spoons!"

Not about to argue with the woman, I shake my head and collect the random things she asked for. I walk into the living room to find Granny all set up with Lucy on the floor. She's put down a blanket and taken the pillows off the couch to create a sort of playmat. The two of them are sitting together, clapping their hands and Granny's singing about stars. Lucy giggles and something inside of me twists at the sound.

Kneeling down, setting the plastic bowls and spoons on the floor. As soon as Lucy spies them, she grabs one of the wood handles and starts banging it on the side of the bowls. Granny cackles, "Smart cookie!" And turns the bowls upside down around Lucy, giving her an entire drum set to work with.

As I look at her playing, all clad in pink, happy as can be, I can't stop the absolute fucking hatred I feel towards the man that let her down. I reach my hand out and gently run my rough finger across her soft face.

So caught up in Lucy, I hadn't noticed Francine was downstairs until I happened to look up and see her standing in the doorway. She's back in her clothes from yesterday. Crouched down, my view starts at her narrow bare feet and works up her form fitting black pants, over her sweater, and to her face. Her hair is damp and pulled back in a braid. She's staring at me in return with an expression I can't place.

I raise my brow, "All set?"

Her gaze turns to Lucy and she crawls down on the blanket. When she sees her, Lucy squeals, "Mama!" and excitedly climbs onto Franny's lap. I have never seen a more beautiful woman than the way she's looking at Lucy right now.

"I'm not sure I should leave her," Franny says, her nose tucked in Lucy's hair.

"Poppycock!" Granny admonishes. "She'll be just fine here with me. Now, get going!"

I kiss Granny on the cheek and stand up. "Yes, ma'am." And put my hand out for Franny. She peers up at me and goddamn, those are bedroom eyes if I've ever seen 'em.

Kissing the top of Lucy's head, Franny sets her down on the blanket and grabs my offered palm. Pulling her from the floor, her body rises up against mine, slightly brushing up my chest as she stands.

And looking down at her, I swear I hear her breath hitch

in our closeness.

Without a word, I pull her hand through the room, to the kitchen and out the back door. We've got shit to do.

SEVEN
A LITTLE MORE... REFINED

Standing in the middle of the aisle at Montgomery Ward, Franny's got her hands on her hips in defiance.

"Pick a coat," I tell her again.

She doesn't move. Just shakes her head. "Butch, I'm fine. I don't need a coat."

Cursing, I reach over and grab the thick blue one on the rack and matching mittens, throwing them in the shopping cart. Ignoring her glare, I walk past her.

This is how it's been since we got here two hours ago. Me telling her to pick out what she needs, her arguing that she doesn't need it, and me choosing one and throwin' it in the cart. Thankfully the place is dead due to last night's weather, so we've pretty much had the store to ourselves.

Montgomery Ward is one of those "buy it all here" places. From household appliances, clothes, electronics, to tools; it's a one-stop-shop for whatever shit you need with the exception of food.

We've made it through the kid stuff, her throwing a tantrum when I told her we were buying a playpen - Granny's orders, and are now working our way, slowly, through the women's clothing. With boots, socks, pants, and shirts in the cart, plus the coat I just picked out, all we have left is one last section.

And I pick up on the moment Franny realizes the department we are approaching as she trips in her short step. Once we're in the middle of the lacy bras and panties, I give her a wicked grin and tease, "Shall I pick out what I prefer here as well, sweetheart?"

Those baby blues are huge when she shakes her head no, disappearing into the racks of unmentionables.

She may be stubborn as hell, but I can tell I get under her skin. And that gives me immense satisfaction. Cause she most definitely gets under mine.

Smirking, I rest my forearms across the shopping cart handle and lean my neck forward, letting my head drop down. It's been a long two days and I'm looking forward to kicking my feet up in front of the fire tonight with a beer. Or doing whatever Franny wants to do. Who'd have thought that I'd be standing here, doing this?

"Butch, I can't decide. Black or white?" I lift my head in the direction of her voice and slip off the handle I'm leaning against. The wheels on the shopping cart shoot forward before I can grab it. I take a deep breath and swallow thickly. Francine is standing in front of me, holding up two very small, very lacy, very sexy, lingerie sets. And she's grinning at me like the damn Cheshire cat.

Clearing my throat, I'm at a loss for words. I rub the back of my neck, trying to snap myself out of it and form a sentence. And by the look on her face, she's loving my struggle.

Gathering my wits, I tuck my hands in my pockets. Making sure to carefully study both options as I approach. When

I'm directly in front of her, close enough to see every one of the freckles that dart across her nose, I tell her, "That's a tough one. I'd need to see them on you before I choose." My head fogs at the thought of her pink skin underneath the delicate flower lacing. So fragile, that I could probably rip them right off her supple body.

Her eyes on my mouth, she leans the slightest bit forward. Our breaths mingle, both of us daring the other to close the distance, when I hear someone say my name from behind and I groan in frustration. "Shit."

"What's wrong?" Francine asks as she pulls back self-consciously, but before I can prepare her for the shit show that's about to go down, Tina's already here.

Dressed like fucking Tiffany and Madonna had a love child, Tina's got a face full of makeup and a big ass bow in her permed black hair. Her bangs are even more teased than the last time I saw her and the huge hoop earrings, paired with a ridiculous amount of necklaces and armful of bracelets, make her a whole hell of a lot to take in. "Omigod Butchy baby, what are you doing here?" And by *here*, she doesn't mean Montgomery Ward. The way she's sizing up Francine, what she means is why am I here with this woman.

"Tina." I acknowledge her, attempting to size up her mood. I've known her since grade school and I've been in and out of her pants at least half that time. Which is really nothing to brag about considering so have most men of marriageable age in Eddington. And everyone knows Tina can be...volatile at times.

"Who's this?" She asks, squinting at Francine as she sizes her up all while simultaneously chomping on the pink bubblegum in her mouth. Everything Tina does is in excess. Even now, standing here right after a historic snowstorm in five layers of shirts, a ridiculous frilly ass skirt and impractical high heel shoes. And with the two of them side by side, Francine's high style and demeanor are distinctly contrast to the woman I had foolishly considered marrying.

Before I can even attempt an introduction, Tina has her attention on the lingerie sets Francine's still holding. Her neon pink press on nails graze down the strap of the white bra. "These are cute." She slants forward and whispers loud enough for me to hear, "But, Butchy prefers red." Tina intentionally gives Francine the once over, and says with a sneer, "And not so vanilla."

"I'll keep that in mind." Francine responds with a cool smile, crossing her arm across her stomach to hide the lingerie. She's about to walk around us, and I reach my hand out to stop her and apologize for Tina's crassness, but she surprises the shit out of me when she pauses, retraces her steps, and looks Tina right in the eye. "Although, maybe he's ready for a different flavor? Perhaps something a little more..." Giving Tina a full body scope in return she ends with, "refined?"

I bark out a laugh and Tina's face turns rageful, stomping her bright pink heel on the carpeted floor, she huffs away.

"She's a peach." Francine says under her breath.

"Listen, I'm sorry about that." I say, grabbing her elbow and turning her towards me.

Purposefully not looking at me, she pulls away from my grip, "Don't worry about it. Let's just finish up so I can get back to Lou Lou."

"Franny, she's an old friend -" But she cuts me off.

"I said don't worry about it. I'm nothing to you. You don't owe me an explanation." Her voice is tight as she tries to get by me again. I block her path, holding on to her upper arms to keep her from fleeing. Pissed off at her indifferent attitude.

Putting my face in hers, I seethe, "You're nothing?"

Her eyes grow wide. "That's not - it's just that -" She lets out a heavy sigh at my raised brow. "I don't know why you're doing this. I don't understand why you're even bothering. If anything, I'm nothing more but a hassle and inconvenience for you."

Now she's gone and pissed me off even more. Gripping her arms, I pull her to her toes and smash her body flush with mine. "Sweetheart, I'm going to tell you this one time and one time only. You are not now, and never will be, a hassle or inconvenience. And I call bullshit that you don't know why I'm doin' this. Because I know damn well you feel what I feel whenever my hands are on you. And we're gonna be explorin' *exactly* what it means." I feel the shudder of her body and I fight the urge to push her against the wall and start my explorations right this damn minute. "Now finish pickin' out your shit, so we can get outta here, yeah?"

"Yeah," she whispers against my face.

I hold her to me a beat longer before I gently release her to her feet and take my place back at the handle of the shopping cart. And wait for her to finish picking out her shit.

And once we've finished our shopping, having stopped at the Food 4 Less to stock up the empty pantry and fridge and grab the toiletries Franny and Lou need, we're back in the truck. The bed is filled to the rim with boxes and bags and we're heading home.

It's a quiet ride, Francine not having said much since the incident at the department store. I've given her space, but I can't stand the silence any longer. "You hungry? We can make a stop at the drive thru on our way home." I pick up on her stiffened spine at the word "home" but ignore it.

"No, thank you. You just got all that food. And I don't have much of an appetite right now." She says to the window, not bothering to look at me.

Not letting her off that easily, I ask, "Is there anything else you need while we're out?"

"No, thank you." Again, answering the glass and not me. Every fucking thing she does is polite and proper. The lady literally oozes class, never once is she not lady-like.

"Damn it. Don't do that, Franny. Don't shut me out."

"What do you want from me, Butch?" Her neck finally turns that pretty head my way. Her face is skeptical.

I stare at the road ahead confused. "I don't want anything from you."

She forces a laugh and mutters, "Every man wants something."

What the fuck? That's it. I'm done. Checking behind me first, I throw on my blinker, pull over onto the brim, and put the Chevy in park. Resting my arm across the steering wheel, I turn my body and look at her. "What the hell does that mean?"

Crossing her arms in front of her, she glares at me. "What do you think it means?"

Biting my teeth together, I say slowly, "If I knew, I wouldn't ask."

"Now that I've seen the kind of *woman* you prefer," her emphasis on *woman* tells me precisely how lady-like she believes Tina to be. "I'm just trying to figure out why you're bothering with someone like me? Do you want to sleep with me? Is that it? Because I can assure you, and save you the trouble by telling you right now, you won't want to be with me."

Utterly fucking stupefied. That's what I am right now. And all I can do is blink at her. "What are you talking about, Franny?"

She throws her hands up in the air. "I can't. I can't be satisfied, okay? My body just doesn't work like that."

"You can't be satisfied." I repeat, drawing out each word slowly in an attempt to sort out what she just said.

Then it hits me like a shitload of bricks. Fuckin' hell. Is she telling me that the asswipe she's been with all this time has never taken her there?

Clenching the fist that's resting over the dashboard, I unbuckle my seatbelt and take in a deep inhale of air. "Unbuckle and come over here."

Her head twitches at my request but she doesn't move. "What? Why?"

"Sweetheart, you either unbuckle yourself and scooch your ass over here or I'll get out, walk around this truck, and push you over myself."

Eyes narrowing, she realizes my threat for the truth it is. Pressing the square button on the seat belt buckle, she slowly moves the black belt off her lap.

Putting her small hand on the space of the bench seat between us, Francine slides over my way, stopping short of where I want her to be. I fix it and pull her the rest of the way over until her thigh is in line with mine. I cup her cheek, forcing her eyes up and stare into those beautiful baby blues. Dammit I wish she hadn't been through what she's been through. I see her mouth open and I put my thumb over her lips before she can talk. Or pull away. Or do whatever the hell she was about to do.

My thumb strokes across those plump kissers and her breath hitches at my touch. Slowly, so slowly, I lean my head forward until my nose nudges down the length of hers, my lips a hair's breadth away. And when our mouths finally connect, we mesh together into a messy tangle of tongue and teeth.

When I hear her moan in need and feel the warmth of her palm when her hand cups my face in return, I groan in response into her mouth.

She breaks the kiss first, gasping for air but I can't stop. My lips kiss and lick down the length of her neck as her hand fists in my hair, my own hand gliding down to her breast. Palming the soft mound that fits perfectly in my hand, I grow frustrated with the layers between us and find my way under her sweater. The skin of her stomach is silky smooth and my nails graze across her flesh, making their way upward to their destination. Reaching the edge of her bra, I pull the thin fabric down, releasing her breast from its confines. Our mouths meet again and our kisses grow frantic. My cock twitches in my pants when Francine arches against the back of the seat, moaning my name as I tweak and pinch her nipple under the weaved fabric of her shirt.

Fuck. I just wanted to kiss her and get her a little aroused to show her how wrong she was. Show her what it was like to be taken care of. I never intended to practically pop off in my fucking pants. And the woman deserves a hell of a lot more than a quickie orgasm in my truck.

Reluctantly releasing her mouth, and fixing her bra, I pull my hand out from her sweater and rest my forehead against hers. Both of us try to catch our breaths. "I think we've proven that your body works *just* like that." I tell her gently as I run my nose down hers again. She lifts her head in response for more.

Dammit. This woman.

"But we've got to stop darlin'. Because when I take you there for the first time Franny, it ain't gonna be in my pickup. And neither one of us will be wearin' clothes." I promise, pressing a kiss between her brows.

"Okay," she whispers, her voice trembling.

Liking this girl just where she's at, I put the truck in gear, and place my arm around her shoulder before I pull back out onto Main Street.

Buckling herself into the middle seat, she sits back and intertwines her fingers through the hand I have draped across her neck.

"I hope Lou Lou's been alright." She says, looking up to me.

I smirk. "I know you don't know Granny Jean very well yet, but Lou Lou's just fine."

"Tell me about her," Francine says.

I take a deep breath. Trying to figure out where to start when describing the woman that made me who I am today. "Well, my parents died in a car accident when I was seven.

And I've lived with her ever since. My dad was her only kid, and his dad, Granny's husband, died over in Germany during the war. She never remarried and after losin' her son too, she devoted her life to raisin' me."

"I'm sorry about your parents, Butch."

"Yeah. It was hard. But Granny made sure I had all I needed."

She laughs a little. "You were probably a handful."

"Sweetheart, I was more than a handful. I owe Granny a helluva lot for putting up with me. Looking back, there were many times she should have just thrown me out on my ass. I was an angry boy that grew into an angry kid that only cared about fighting and fucking.

"The last time I got in trouble, I was given a choice. Either take shop class and do something with myself or get the hell out of town. And seein' as how I had nowhere to go, I signed up for shop. Met Wren, Kurt, and Jax, and stopped puttin' my hands in fists and started gettin' my hands greasy instead." I say, extending my fingers out to accentuate the calluses, stains and cracks.

"Jax is the police officer that helped me the other night?"

"Yep. Best Police Chief the city of Eddington's ever had. Kurt opened KJ's. It's the local dive. I'll take you there sometime soon. And Wren owns Rollin' Right, where your piece of shit car is probably right this minute."

Pulling down on my finger playfully, she huffs, "The car's not that bad!"

"Darlin', it's a piece of shit."

She gets quiet before she asks softly, "How am I going to pay for the repairs?"

Pulling into my driveway, I squeeze her hand, "Let's get to that when it comes to us, yeah?"

"Yeah." Her quiet voice agrees.

In the time it takes me to hop out of the cab, Francine's already made it out of her seat, around the house, and to the back door. Opening the bed of the truck, I gather an arm full of bags and a box of toys.

Francine rushes out the door in a flash. "They're not there!"

"What?" about to head in with the first load, I look around her into the kitchen.

"They're not there! The lights are off and the fire's out. They're not in there, Butch!"

"Sweetheart, take a breath." I set the bags and box down on the kitchen floor right inside the door. "Granny probably walked Lou Lou over to her house." Cocking my chin towards the small white house to the right of us.

"Come on," I tell her over my shoulder, knowing she's already following. "Let's walk over."

She stays close behind as we take the path I shoveled early this morning from my driveway up to Granny's door.

Stepping onto the stoop, I push the front door open and move out of the way to allow Francine to pass by and go into the house. Where, on the middle of the family room floor, Lucy Lou and Sam the spoiled cat are nestled on a blanket. Lucy's arm is draped around the furry orange and white striped tabby, and they're both sound asleep. Granny's sitting cross-legged on the blanket next to them reading a book.

She "shushes" us as we walk in, and Francine puts her

hand over her heart. Clearly once panicked and now relieved about the idea of Lou Lou going missing.

I grab her other hand. "Let's go unpack and do as much as we can while she's out."

Nodding her head, Francine looks at the sleeping baby on the floor one last time and turns to me with a smile. I step out the door and hold it open for her.

She whispers a heartfelt, "Thank you, Jean."

"She's a good girl," Granny tells her quietly before I close the door behind us.

Eight

Atta-Girl

Everything is been unpacked and Francine's fixing dinner downstairs.

Sitting in the spare bedroom that was empty this morning and now is full of empty boxes, little pastel outfits, diapers and toys, I'm trying to set up this death contraption of a playpen.

The damn thing came with instructions that I finally balled up in frustration. Every time I get the sides to lock, the middle juts up like a fucking folding bridge.

I hear a light giggle that runs straight to my groin. "Still at it?"

Francine is standing in the doorway, leaning against the jamb. She looks calm and comfortable, holding the crumpled directions.

"The instructions were useless."

A sly grin crosses her face. "Need a hand?"

I chuckle, "If I can't get it, you won't -" Before I finish my sentence she's pulled the two sides up at the same time, locking the bottom in place. Pulling up on the other two sides, she lifts them up swiftly, pulling the entire damn contraption off the floor and they click.

"There." She says, swiping her hands across each other. Not paying any mind to my gaping mouth, she asks, "Ready to eat? We made lasagna."

Feeling like a dolt, I stand with my brows and arms crossed. "We?"

An easy smile forms on her lips, "Yeah, me and my little helper. She helped stir the sauce."

Now I raise my brow. I may have only been around Lucy Lou a short time, but she's a busy body that can barely take five steps without tumbling. I can't imagine her being much help at much of anything.

Laughing, Francine says, "Well, she ate the cheese. That counts, right?"

"Sure does," I say, following her out into the hallway and down the stairs. Our footsteps echo through the empty hall.

Walking into the kitchen, my nose is assaulted by a magnificent mix of garlic and tomato. Lucy's strapped into the booster seat we picked up today, slamming her tiny yellow spoon against her tiny yellow plate, her face covered in pasta sauce. The sight makes me smile.

"Hey Lou Lou," I coo as I walk over to the sink to wash my hands, telling Francine, "It smells amazing."

Waiting at the table, she sounds almost nervous. "I hope it's good. It's been a long time since I've made anything like this."

My hand brushes against her back as I pass by. Ever since our moment in the truck, I find it hard to be near her and not touch her. "I'm sure it's great, sweetheart."

I pull my chair out and sit next to Lucy. The kid looks like she's wearing more food than she's eating.

Francine leans over and spoons a square of lasagna onto my plate.

"Garlic bread?" She asks, reaching across the table to hand me the basket.

"Sure," I say, choosing a butter-covered breadstick from the top of the pile.

"Salad?" The big clear glass bowl of freshly made salad in her hands.

Picking up the tongs, I claw a bunch of lettuce and cucumber into the edges and drop it on my plate. "Thanks."

I've got the fork full of hot, steamy lasagna halfway to my mouth when Francine asks, "Can I get you anything else?"

Realizing she's still standing next to me, I put the fork down and look up at her. "Franny, darlin', if I need anything else, I've got two legs and two arms that work just fine. Now, sit down and eat with us while it's hot."

My foot connects with the legs of her chair and kicks it out. Looking taken aback, she sits down.

I'm digging into my food while she's making her own plate. Her first bite is almost to her mouth when Lucy throws her milk cup down to the floor. Dropping her fork still full of food, Francine pushes her chair out to stand and pick it up.

"Sit." I tell her, reaching down and picking up the yellow cup that matches the new dinner set we bought today for Lou Lou.

Putting the cup on the tray in front of her, Lucy Lou screams and claps her hands. Chuckling at her excitement, I ask, "You like that, huh?"

I'm rewarded with more clapping and an even bigger

toothless smile. I tap her midget nose and turn back to the table to find Francine sitting with her hands in her lap. Staring at me.

"I don't know how to thank you. To - to truly thank you for everything you've done for us." Her voice is quivering and the telltale sign of water collecting in her eyes leads me to believe she's about to lose it.

"Hey," I say quietly, cupping her face with my hand and brushing my thumb under her eye where the droplet is forming. "None of that.

"Franny, I'm not a man that does anything I don't want to. And I'm also not a man that gives my time to people I don't want to give my time to. What I'm saying is, you wouldn't be here, sittin' at my table, if I didn't want you here."

"And if you decide you no longer want us around?"

Her words damn near break my heart. What sort of people has she had in her life to make her feel so dispensable? I suppose I'm treading thin water here. I've never been one to wax poetic and I'm not a liar. So, I decide to lay it straight.

"I can't tell the future. But I believe there's a higher power at play and I don't think it's a coincidence that you've come into my life. Twice now. So as far as what happens next? All I know is I like the direction we're headin', and I have a feeling we both know where we're goin'.

"Now, eat, sweetheart."

Picking her fork back up, she smiles and takes her bite.

"I'm lookin' forward to finishing what we started in the pickup today, too." I tell her, raising my eyebrows right before I put my own bite into my mouth. I laugh when her face turns red and she chokes a bit on her lasagna.

Throughout the remainder of the meal, I pick up Lucy Lou's cup from the floor about a hundred more times. And we laugh our asses off when Lou Lou lets out a belch that would put the grown men chugging beers at KJ's to shame.

Speaking of which, the boys are expecting me at the pub tonight. And after the past few days, I could definitely pound back a few beers.

I told Francine that I'd clean up the dishes and she took the baby upstairs for a bath. So, here I am like a domestic housewife washing and drying plates. In all the time I've lived here, I don't think I have ever used this many pots and pans at the same time. Hell, I didn't even know I owned some of these.

"Well, let's see how this goes." Francine says, walking in and grabbing a dish towel. I notice the front of her shirt is wet from bathing Lucy. I can just imagine that kid in water. She probably flounces around like a fish. She's going to love the swimming hole down at the park. It's been years since I've been there, but considering how excited she gets over a wooden spoon and Tupperware, I'm looking forward to seeing that tiny face light up at the site of all that water.

"She in bed already?" I ask.

Picking up the stock pot I just scrubbed and rinsed, Francine starts drying it off. "Yeah. We never really had a good schedule with me working so much and Lou Lou at the sitters all the time. And when I wasn't working, I wanted to spend time with her." There's a pause before she says, "I hated the life I made her live."

"Don't do that. Don't beat yourself up. That's a happy girl you got there. You did what you could with what you had and you loved her. That's all she needed."

Clearly wanting to change the subject, she takes a deep breath and grabs the next pan. "Are you sure we shouldn't take some food over to Jean? There's plenty of leftovers."

Rubbing the soapy washcloth over the last drinking glass, I shake my head. "Nah. Tonight's her big card night. She's got all the girls over and they're busy eating cheesecake and drinking wine. I can take her a plate tomorrow."

Finishing up the last of the dishes, I throw down the rag into the empty sink. "So, I'm going to go out for a bit. Meet up with the guys at KJ's. You good here?"

"Oh! Um, yeah. We're fine." She answers a little bit hesitantly.

"Good. I'll uh - I'll see you later, yeah?" Not sure why we are both acting awkward as shit, but also not really wanting to stick around to find out.

Grabbing my leather jacket from the chair, I head out. Closing the back door behind me, I almost look back through the window to see if she's still there, but I don't.

My track record proves I'm not the best at relationships. And if she was still standing there, would I just stay?

I place the truck in reverse and back out of the driveway before I can find out.

NINE

HI, DARLIN'

Dammit. Switching from beer to whisky was a bad fucking idea.

The boys have finally stopped drilling me about my houseguests and now we're talking about the Harley coming out next year.

"They're callin' it the Heritage Softail," Wren says after the last (and final, for me anyway) round of shots.

"You gonna get one?" Jax asks him. We all know Wren saves his money like a fiend. He rarely spends it, and when he does, it's usually on something for the garage. Or to help Kurt help the girls that come in.

But the way he's been talking about this Harley since he read about it in a magazine a few months ago, we all know he's going to splurge.

And why the hell not? The guy works his ass off, he deserves it.

"I don't know," Wren answers Jax. We all chuckle. Knowing he's full of shit.

"You boys need anything else?" Gemma asks, pressing her tits together in front of us. She's been eyeing me all night and my eyes have been trying to avoid it.

"We're good Gem," Kurt tells her.

But instead of walking away, she singles me out. "And what about you Butch? Can I get you anything?"

"Nah. Thanks." Keeping my eyes on the empty shot glass in my hand.

Still not getting the hint, she leans farther forward, her straight blonde hair practically on my arm. "I'm off soon. You want to come upstairs tonight?"

I look up at her for the first time since I got here and feel like a total fucking slimeball. I know she was talking about going back home months ago, right before I started screwing around with her. And I know she stayed because of it.

"Not tonight, Gemma." I say quietly even though the guys are all busy acting like they're not listening.

I stand up. "I'm going to piss and head off," I tell the boys, slapping Wren on the shoulder as I pass by him.

"You better sneak in quiet!" Kurt laughs. "Wouldn't want to wake up the wifey and kid!"

All the guys laugh in chorus.

When I finish in the bathroom, I walk out to find Gemma leaning against the wall in the back hall. She's taken off her KJ's apron. Her tight shirt showing off her ample tits. "There you are," She says, pushing off the wood paneling and right against me.

"Gemma, I -" My words are cut off with her mouth. Her arm wraps around my neck and she pushes my head down farther to hers, backing me up against the huge Pall Mall poster.

Her body grinds against mine and I grab her thigh, lifting it up against my waist to get better friction on my dick.

We are lip locked in a pretty hot and heavy kiss when she says, "Let's go upstairs."

I come to my senses. Fuck. What am I doing?

Putting down her thigh, I take a step away to create distance between us. "Gemma, I can't. I'm sorry. I never should have -"

"It's the woman at your house, right?"

Of course, she would have heard the guys riding my dick about it all night.

"It's complicated. You're a great girl, I just, I can't do this with you anymore."

Crossing her arms in front of her, she says, "I understand." Skirting by me, she begins to rush up the back staircase to her apartment.

"Gemma, wait!" Following her, I go up three steps to catch her and pull her into my arms, hugging her tightly. "I'm sorry. You deserve better than this."

Taking a deep breath, she pulls out of my hug and gives me a weak smile. "I'll see you later, Butch." Taking the last few steps up and disappearing at the top.

I walk out the back door to avoid the "walk of shame" in front of the guys. No doubt those assholes knew Gemma was waiting for me.

So lost in thought over the woman and child in my house, Gemma, my life in general, I wind up sitting here in the parking lot for almost half an hour before I snap out of it and drive home. I don't know much, but I know I'm not going to solve any of my problems in the parking lot of a bar in the middle of the night.

Kurt would lose his shit if he knew I did actually sneak

into the house. Trying to be as quiet as possible, I take off my boots at the doormat and make a straight trajectory to the couch in the family room.

"You're back," Francine says, standing in between the kitchen and dining room.

Shit. "I was trying to be quiet. Sorry for waking you up."

Stepping all the way in the room, I see she's wearing one of my t-shirts again. "You didn't wake me up." Opening the cupboard, she stands on her toes and the shirt lifts in the back. There's just enough light that I can see the bottom of her panty-covered ass.

Francine gets a glass and fills it up at the sink. "I was just thirsty." She says, taking a sip of water.

"I like you in my shirt," I growl, unable to keep my mouth shut. Dammit. Yep. The whisky shots were a bad idea.

She's putting the glass down on the counter right as I say it, and she somehow manages to knock it off the edge. The glass hits the floor and shatters.

"Shoot!" she yells.

"No big deal." I assure her, quickly walking over the sink. I grab the towel off the dishrack and both of us kneel down. Our heads practically touching, I lay the towel on the floor and start putting the larger pieces on top of it. Francine picks one up but drops it and jerks her hand back, the glass slicing the tip of her pointer finger. "Ow!" She cries, sucking on the cut.

God damn. Those lips.

I cover the hand at her mouth with mine and when those doe eyes look up to me, I realize that I'm lost. I'm lost to the girl buying Lucky Charms and chunky peanut butter in the middle of the night. I'm lost to the woman strong enough to leave a shitty situation with nothing but the clothes on her back to find safety. And I lied when I said I didn't know what the future held. Because I know for damn certain that these two girls aren't leaving.

I slowly pull on her hand, watching her finger slide out from her mouth. And keeping our eyes locked, I bring her hand up and push her finger between my lips. My tongue licks across her cut and I taste a little of the baby shampoo she used on Lucy Lou upstairs earlier. Eyes on my mouth, her eyelids half-close in desire and her chest heaves as her breath increases.

Pulling her finger out, I tug her hand towards me, bringing her forward until we meet over the pile of broken glass.

I trace her lips with my tongue. "Open for me, darlin'," I whisper against her mouth.

And when she parts those plump pink lips like I asked, I growled into her mouth, my tongue dipping and diving, gliding against the roof of her mouth, her teeth and her tongue. Losing myself in her welcoming warmth.

She sighs against me, leaning farther in, pushing her mouth harder against mine. Craving more and matching my own hunger. I feel the sweat bead on my forehead, further evidence that we are about to ignite into a burst of flames.

My legs are trembling as I attempt to remain kneeling and consume her at the same time. Abruptly, I stand, pulling her up with me. Melding our mouths together, I back her up against the fridge. My body pressed solidly against hers, my fingers thread into her hair and pull her head sideways, giving me full access to her neck where I lick my way to her ear. Tasting her sugary candy flavor. "Francine," I whisper as I bite her lobe. She moans in response to her name and my hand finds its way under the shirt she's wearing. Tired of having so much between us, I grasp the hem and pull it over her head as her arms raise up and I slide the sleeves up and off.

Dropping back down to my knees, I kiss across her bare chest and her hands knot into my hair. I worship her, breathing her name against her skin over and over.

As I lick and suck her peaked nipple, blowing and kissing as I cross the small expanse to lavish the second one, she moans my name. Her hands tug on my hair, telling me she wants my mouth on hers.

So, I work my way back on my feet, my tongue never leaving her skin until it's inside her mouth. My hand roams across her bare stomach and circles over the top of her panties. Testing and teasing, inching down, getting closer and closer to her pussy with each round.

Arching against the fridge, Francine is mewling in anticipation. The tips of my fingers graze soft, curly hair, and I growl in desire, attacking her mouth at the same time I push my fingers the last inch into her wet folds.

Inhaling at the contact, her voice is sultry and wild when she calls out, "God! Yes!"

But my hand freezes when I hear the high-pitched cry coming from upstairs.

"No, no, no, no." Francine whispers, her voice on the verge of tears of her own.

Resting my head against her bare chest, I pull my fingers out from her underwear. Trying to catch my breath and regain my self-control.

"You better go darlin'." I tell her roughly. Knowing if she stays here another second, I'll start right where we left off and never stop.

Reaching down, I pick up the balled shirt off the floor, pulling the sleeves right side out. Holding it out, she grabs it from my hands and quickly shoves it on, running her fingers through her hair.

Starting to rush out of the room, she stops and looks at me questioningly, as if she's worried I'm upset that we were interrupted.

I grab her face and give her a fast, deep kiss before I turn her around and gently push her back towards the doorway. Encouraging her to go soothe Lou Lou. And when she's upstairs and the crying has quieted to a tired whine, I'm still standing in the kitchen. My hands on my waist, and my head tipped up with my eyes closed.

Fuck. I don't think a bucket full of ice water could have made my balls bluer than what they are right now. Two times in one night they were denied a bust.

I finish cleaning up the glass shards, turn the lights off, and check that the door's locked.

Cutting through the living room, heading to check the front door, I damn near shit my pants when my foot kicks into something that starts glowing fluorescent green and playing screechy tunes. Picking up the worm-shaped doll, I look everywhere for the button. "Damn thing doesn't turn off." I mutter to myself in the dark and toss the creepy toy onto the couch. That sucker's not going to help any kid go to sleep.

Practically tiptoeing upstairs, I take a cold shower and brush my teeth.

My curiosity gets the best of me on my way back downstairs and I peek my head into my bedroom. Lying face to face, Francine's holding the little one in the crook of her arm. Lucy's brown curls are springing in ringlets all over her head and she's covered from neck to toe in fuzzy pink pajamas.

It's so quiet, I can hear the soft snoring coming from Lou Lou's nose and I smile.

Gently tucking Francine's legs under the sheets, I pull the blankets up and make sure they're both covered. Francine moans in her sleep, pulling Lucy even tighter to her body.

I don't know how long I stand here ogling them, but I do know I could do it till morning. I feel a strong sense of satisfaction that they're both resting soundly in my bed, knowing that they sleep so hard because they know they're safe.

Quietly closing the door behind me, I head down to spend another long night on the couch.

I don't know how long I laid here, looking out the window at the snow falling slowly from the sky, but I must have eventually found sleep. Because the next thing I know, I've got a pair of tiny hands smacking my face, babbling and blowing bubbles from her mouth while she bounces and dances, holding onto the couch, and my face, for support.

Francine is rushing in, apologizing and pulling Lucy into her arms, as I stretch and sit up. "Don't be sorry. There are worse things than getting woke up by a pretty face," I tell her, taking in Francine in her new outfit.

I recognize it from yesterday's shopping trip. The blue

shirt is one I picked out when she was playing stubborn. I can see now that I was right - the color matches her eyes. And the jeans that are hugging those hips just right are ones she pulled off the rack when I threatened to buy one of each style.

Her brown curly hair frames her face, and I notice she's wearing makeup. Nothing heavy like the shit Tina cakes on, but a light covering on her face that shimmers in the morning light but, to my delight, still lets those freckles shine through.

Her pink, glossy lips are pursed, and when I finish my perusal, I find that she's watching me watching her.

Remembering having her writhing in my hands last night. Recalling the soft moans and sighs when I touched her, when my finger slipped right into her, I feel absolutely feral this morning. "Hi darlin'."

"Good morning." She smiles shyly, as though she can read the dirty thoughts floating through my head. Then again, the way my eyes are raking her over, I'm sure it's obvious what I'm thinking of.

"There's fresh coffee. You want a cup?" She offers.

"Absolutely." I answer. Never one to turn down a hot cup of joe. Plus, it'll do wonders for the massive headache I'm sporting right now.

"Do you have plans this week?" She asks over her shoulder, carrying Lucy on her hip.

I told the boys I'd be taking a couple days off, and for as much as I'd love to stay in the house with the girls longer, and get to know them better, I really should make a trip into the garage and touch base with the crew. I'm sure Joe has everything under control, but it's still my ship to sail.

"I think I'll head into work later this morning. I can run to the store on my way home if you need anything?"

"Maybe just more milk?" She says, opening the cabinet to pull a box of cereal down. Lucy's pulling on the collar of her shirt and babbling.

I take a sip of coffee and nod my head. "Got it. I'll leave you the garage number in case you think of anything else. You can call me anytime there. And if I'm not in, the boys can get me on the radio."

"Alright," she answers as she straps Lucy into the seat.

We finish breakfast together enjoying light conversation and a few laughs. And when I leave for work, she's waiting at the door with Lucy, a paper bag lunch in her hands. I say my goodbyes, running my finger down her cheek, and then Lou Lou's, and walk out thinking that a man could definitely get used to this lifestyle.

The next few days pass by just the same - minus the making out at the fridge before bed, unfortunately. Waking up in the morning on the couch, enjoying my coffee while she feeds Lucy, me headin' out for work, her waiting for me at the door with a packed lunch.

With every day that passes, I feel Franny growing more comfortable. More sure of herself. And I enjoy her company greatly. I've noticed little things about her. Her clumsiness and her style. She's formal even when she's relaxed. She isn't like any woman I've ever known.

The house has never been cleaner and dinner's always ready by the time I get home. I've come to look forward to the excitement on Lou Lou's face when I walk in the back door.

If I don't hear from Francine by noon, I call the house to check in. Mostly because I just want to hear her voice; I'm finding I miss her when I'm gone.

I've been giving her space, allowing her time to sort through what she wants. What she needs. Waiting for her to figure out that the answer to those questions is sleeping on the couch in the family room every damn night.

Last night, waiting for sleep to claim me on the couch, I decided I'd take her out. Granny had been stopping in during the day to say hi to the baby or drop off freshly made cookies. Whatever excuse she can come up with to hold the baby and get to know Francine. She'd be more than happy to keep Lucy for the night. Hell, she'd be fucking thrilled.

So, observing Franny move around the kitchen this morning, I decide now is as good a time as any when she asks me, "Are you working late tonight?"

"Nope." I tell her as she straps Lucy into her booster. "And I'm takin' you out."

Francine's hands still on the buckles of the seat for a split second, but I catch it. Turning back around to grab the box of Cheerios on the counter, she asks, "Like, a date?" It was a solid attempt at sounding casual and indifferent to my meaning, but there is something about her that I find easy to read.

"You can call it a date. You can call it drinks. You can call it whatever you want, darlin'. All I care is that at the end of the night, you'll be callin' my name."

The dry cereal in her hands spills and scatters all over the floor.

Satisfied with her reaction, I cross my foot over my leg and take a long sip of coffee.

But when she's down on her knees, scooping up the circles, I hear her exclaim quietly, "Why does it seem like I'm always on the floor when I'm with you?" And I let out a barking laugh.

Apparently, my loud voice seems funny to Lou Lou, because she starts slamming her hands on her tray, belly giggling right alongside me. And looking at her tiny face, her curly hair in a riot all over her head as she bounces up and down, those perfect little eyes closed tight and squeals of delight coming from her wide-open mouth, I bust up even more. It's only a beat before we're joined by Francine, her peals of sweet giggles sounding through the kitchen.

"That girl's laughter is contagious," I tell her, still chuckling under my breath.

Throwing herself into her chair, her face still split wide with a blinding smile, Francine lets out a loud sigh. "It's been a long time since I've laughed like that."

Looking at her sitting there - so god damn beautiful- I shake my head in shame. That asswipe Stephen had solid gold in his hands and he absolutely fucking squandered it.

I've always been one to know a good thing when I see it. My face grows serious and I tell her, "Sweetheart, you stick with me, and I'll do everything I can to get you to laugh just so I can see that gorgeous smile all the damn time."

Her cheeks flush red, but instead of turning away or looking down or doing anything to deflect from the words she's not accustomed to hearing, she brushes her hair behind her ear and gifts me with the biggest, sunshiniest fucking smile yet.

Shifting forward, I run my finger down her cheek and whisper, "Atta-girl."

TEN
You Were Worth The Wait

I told her we'd leave at seven.

It's now 7:37, and I've yet to see her since she disappeared upstairs to get ready. I walked Lou Lou over to Granny's about an hour ago and was quickly shooed out by the old lady that had been anxiously waiting to get her hands on the baby since I'd called her this morning and asked her to babysit.

Before I dropped off the little one- and the three bags of shit Francine had packed for her- and showered and changed my dirty t-shirt and jeans into a clean t-shirt and jeans, I told Francine not to bother getting too dolled up. Where we're going doesn't require fancy clothes or reservations. To be honest, I've never been anywhere that had a dress code and needed my name on a list.

I look at my Rolex one more time and sigh, tapping my fingers on my jeans. I've never been good at waiting. Standing up, I stretch and head to the kitchen to grab a beer from the fridge. Cracking it open, I walk back into the living room and plop myself down on the couch, putting my feet on the coffee table.

Something falls onto the floor upstairs and I hear Francine

curse. I snicker at her clumsiness. She's always dropping something or breaking something or knocking something over. It's pretty fucking adorable.

Swallowing a swig of Coors, I call upstairs. "You take much longer and we'll be drinking beer and eating leftovers here at home!"

I'm taking Francine to KJ's. Wednesday is wing night and as good a night as any to get out of the house. And it doesn't hurt that my buddy Kurt has a bona fide chef working in his kitchen. He may call it a pub, but the food that comes out of that back room is damn good. Better than any restaurant in Eddington. Of course, the big wigs in town wouldn't deign to show their faces in such a low-class establishment, even though Kurt is as high-class as they come. So, the good grub is our little secret.

The sound of shoes on the stairs has me turning my head, waiting for Francine to appear around the corner and into the room I'm waiting in. And when she does, I swallow my beer hard.

Jesus.

She's wearing an emerald green sweater dress that fits her body tightly, accentuating her amazing curves. The dress stops just above her kneecaps and her legs are sheer in tights underneath and partly covered by sexy black boots.

"I'm sorry it took so long." She says quietly, adjusting the high neckline like she's nervous of what I'll think or say. The dress is simple, no patterns or distracting shit. She doesn't need it anyway.

"Turn around."

Keeping her hands on her neck, she slowly moves in a

circle.

The back of the dress is cut in a low V and her curly hair is down, brushing just past the back of her neck.

Taking her all in, I wait until she's finished her spin and is facing me again before I whistle. "Darlin', you were worth the wait."

"What?" She asks, fidgeting with her sleeve now.

"I think you heard me," I tell her, stepping towards her slowly. "But if you need to hear more, I'm happy to oblige."

Wrapping my hand around the side of her neck, my thumb pushes her chin up as I look down on her lightly powdered face. "You are fucking beautiful, Franny."

"Thanks," she whispers, her face so close to mine that I can smell her mint toothpaste. I imagine how that shiny gloss tinting her lips like a strawberry would look smeared all over her and me.

"I want to kiss you, sweetheart. But if I start kissin' you, we won't be leaving the house tonight. And you won't be wearing that dress much longer."

Looking into my eyes, I know she can see the desire and truth in my dark expression.

"Okay, Butch," she quietly answers.

"God damn," I blow my breath over her head and grab her hand, pulling her out of the house before I can change my mind.

Walking into KJ's, we're greeted like Norm on Cheers. The bar takes up the entire left side of the room and the kitchen is on the right, with a serving window cut out of the wall. The wood paneling darkens the space, but the orange and yellow glass pendants scattered across the ceiling add enough light to make it comfortable. A half dozen round tables and chairs are in the center and against the back wall, next to the pool table, sits the jukebox and cigarette machines.

KJ's might be considered the town dive, but it's clean and Kurt takes care of the girls that work the bar. Most of them come in here after falling on hard times, knowing Kurt will give them a job. Typically, the women only stay for a while, and then move on to bigger and better things - a true testament for what Kurt offers while they're here. A chance to land on their feet again. That's exactly what Gemma's doing working here. She escaped an abusive relationship and rents the room above the bar from Kurt. And from what Kurt says, she's just about ready to pack up and head out of town.

All things considered, that's probably for the best. And, looking around, I don't see her. She must be off tonight which is a bit of a relief. I'm not sure I'm ready to explain that to Franny yet. Not that the arrangement between Gemma and I will ever happen again, but I'm not proud of the fact that it adds more corrosion to my already tarnished name.

"I take it these are all your friends?" Francine giggles while I'm holding her hand, walking towards the bar where I see Wren nursing a beer.

"Yep."

Pulling her up beside me, I nod at Wren still in his mechanic uniform, He's unbuttoned the coverall and it's draped around his waist, revealing the black t-shirt that's as much of his daily uniform as my white ones. The ornery smirk on his face means he's already seen us. Wren has always been the looker of the four of us boys. Like a blonde Tom Cruise with his clean-cut looks, short blonde hair and blue eyes. Until you get to his arms and hands. Scarred, burned, and stained from working under hot car hoods for the past twenty years; he may look pretty, but he's not afraid to get his hands dirty.

"So, this is your situation?" He asks as I approach. Referring to our cryptic phone conversation the other day while I was in the kitchen with the girls, even though he already knows exactly who this is.

Squinting my eyes at him in warning, I say, "*This* is Franny." Ignoring his growing smartass smirk, I look at Francine. "Franny, this asshole is my best friend, Wren."

"It's nice to meet you." She says, immediately putting her hand out to shake his. Wren looks down at the delicate fingers with perfectly painted pink nails in mild disbelief before gently sliding his oil blemished palm in hers. It's no secret that when you work a blue-collar job, women like Francine are typically less than enamored with the grubby skin and grimy clothes that accompany it. Especially around here.

"The pleasure's mine," he answers, looking from Francine to me and back to her again. "I believe it's your piece of shit Pacer I have up on my lifters back at the shop?"

"It's not a piece of shit..." Francine begins to answer.

"Darlin', I told you. It's a piece of shit," I tell her, smiling at her stubbornness and inability to admit the obvious. Kissing the side of her head, I motion for her to sit down on the high barstool next to Wren, ignoring the surprise on both of their faces.

She sits down gracefully, tucking her dress under her and

crossing her legs like a real lady. "So, how much are the repairs going to cost?" Francine asks Wren.

Making eye contact with me above Francine's head, he gathers what he needs to know from my expression and tells her, "Not sure yet. Waitin' on parts. Pacers are built with a hodge podge of auto parts, so we gotta order out the replacement pieces."

Which will no doubt be expensive, and I don't want Franny worrying about that yet. Not until we've worked out the long-term plan. Or at least until I've shared my long-term plan.

Taking my seat on the other side of Francine, I spot Kurt walking out of the kitchen. He wears his hair long on the top and right now it's down in his eyes, covering the naturally tan skin of his face. His red KJ's Pub shirt is unbuttoned down his neck, untucked from his black jeans, and he's wiping his hands off on a rag. He must have been working on the big old commercial oven again. "Do you serve beers here or just let people mill around on their asses for free?"

Chuckling, he yells back, "When's the last time you paid for a beer, Sundance?"

That earned a raucous roar of laughter from all the regulars throughout the bar, and I roll my eyes. Joker won't drink or smoke, but he has no problem being a dick.

"Jax here yet?" Kurt asks, starting to fill up glasses of beer behind the bar.

"Yep," Wren says, pointing the rim of his glass towards the door. "There's our respected Police Chief now."

Jax looks every bit the Chief of Eddington Police Department walking towards us. Even his patriarchal face, military cut black hair, and bright green eyes fit the bill.

"Jesus, how many times we gotta tell you to change before walking in here?" Wren asks, taking a swig of his beer. "You make us look like a bunch of sissy straight-laced Susans palin' around with the big head honcho."

"That was a fuck of a lot of words that made no sense, Wren. I think you've been inhaling fuel fumes in your garage again," Jax answers, grabbing one of the beer glasses that Kurt is sliding down the bar top.

Winking at Francine, he astutely says, "I see you're still around."

I put my hand on her back, "Franny, you've already met Jax. And the guy behind the bar with a toothpick in his mouth is Kurt. These three are my ride or die buds."

Francine offers her hand to Kurt, smiling and knocking him off his feet just like she did me. I can see it in his eyes. I put my arm around Franny and Kurt looks at me with a knowing grin. Yeah, I know I'm being territorial you fucker. Don't goad me.

Franny asks him, "Do you have White Zinfandel, by chance?" Why am I not surprised she's not a beer drinker?

Twisting the toothpick around in his mouth, he's smiling so deep his dimples are showing. "Let me see what I can find for you," he tells her, turning around to the bar.

And when she extends her hand to Jax, Mr. Miami Vice goes into full detective mode asking her all sorts of questions. Some of which I already knew, but others I didn't.

"Franny? Is that short for something?"

"Francine," she answers.

"Of course, and where are you from?"

Kurt slides a glass filled up with something dark. "No wine, but this is a Long Island Tea. I think you'll like it." He winks at her again before heading down to the other side of the bar for a refill.

"Thank you," she says, taking a short sip from her straw. She clears her throat and answers Jax. "Clarks Grove."

"Ah, yes. Well, Francine from Clarks Grove, welcome to Eddington."

"Thank you."

"How long are you planning on staying in our podunk town?" He asks, taking a swallow of Coors.

"Well, to be honest, I don't know. Lou Lou and I are very grateful for everything Butch has done for us, but we couldn't possibly impose much longer."

Kurt has just walked back to stand at the bar with us, the juke box in the back has started its preprogrammed playlist for the night.

"Lou Lou?" Wren asks, brows raised.

The fact that she thinks she's imposing agitates me to no end. So, I answer Wren, but keep my eyes on Francine. "Lou Lou is Franny's little girl, Lucy Lou, I've told you all about. Who is staying with me, along with her mother, and you all already know that," I tell the nosy-ass guys. Then I look right at her. "And I promise you, there is *no* imposition."

Franny blushes and takes a sip of her hard tea to avoid my stare. Dammit, I thought we'd figured all this out already.

"So, you were married?" Jax asks, continuing his after-hours interrogation.

Choking on her drink, Franny coughs and shakes her head vehemently. "No! No. Not married. It's just me and Lou

Lou."

"No family around here?" Jax prods. Even though I should tell him to shut up, I have to admit that I'm just as interested in a lot of these answers.

"No. The Whitmore's hail from Clarks Grove and England," she snorts, "and nowhere else."

"Hm," Jax breathes and we all chuckle.

Francine looks around, confused. "What? What's so funny?"

"Sweetheart, even your name is snooty." I break it to her.

"I am *not* snooty," she retorts, sitting up higher, brushing her hair off her shoulders, and raising that pert nose into the air. In turn causing all of us to bust out laughing again.

"No darlin', you're not snooty. But everything about you is high-class. The way you walk, the way you talk, the way you sit...even your damn name screams money."

"That's not true!" She cries out, looking completely scandalized by my observation.

And when she looks from face to face of the four men surrounding her, and we all avoid her eyes and drink our beer quietly, she realizes we all think just that.

Clearing her throat, she shimmies higher in her seat and looks at Kurt, "I think I will take that beer, please."

Rapping his knuckles on the bar, he nods his head and smiles, "Yes, ma'am." And heads to the tap.

Putting my hand on her back, I lean towards her, "Darlin', you don't have to drink a beer to prove you're not snooty."

Turning those bedroom eyes to me, she presses even closer to me, so close I find a heart-shaped freckle right under her left eye that I'd never noticed before. "I'm drinking a beer because I *want* to. I'm not *high-class*, I don't *scream money*, and I'm *not* snooty," and flips her curly, candy-smelling hair right in my face.

Damn, my girl is snooty. And stubborn as hell.

Her beer, which she managed to gag down eventually, was followed by a round of tequila shots on Wren. Followed by baskets of wings and another round of tequila shots on Kurt. The final round of shots on Jax, that I forbid Franny from taking due to the fact that she was now officially best friends with all my childhood pals and even kissed Mr. Cop on the cheek for "saving her in that snowstorm." Which I thought was bullshit considering *I* was the one that drove out in that shit weather to pick her up. And she just willingly offers *him* a kiss?

Jax must have seen the look of wrath in my eyes because he hooted his ass off and punched my shoulder. And when I went to the bathroom, Franny apparently stuck her tongue out at my retreating back and took the shot anyway.

So now, I'm wrangling a very drunk, and very giggly, Francine out of the bar.

She has formerly met and said goodbye to everyone in the bar three times, hugged my boys, and offered to work for Kurt in order to pay off her bill to Wren. And I made it clear to both her and Kurt, that the answer to that was a definite hell no. A woman like Franny has no business working in a bar. Even if it is a respectable place like KJ's.

And because apparently fate thinks it's fucking hilarious to mess with me, as soon as we're finally on our way out, the big heavy door opens in front of us, blowing in a gust of cold air and a very done up Tina.

Her overly made-up face goes from happy to murderous in a mere second when she looks from me to Francine.

"Butchy baby," she says around her bright red lipstick, "I figured you'd be here, but do you really need to bring your poor charity case with you everywhere you go?

Granny's old bitty card friends no doubt got the skinny last night and spent their day playing phone tag, relaying the latest juicy gossip about bad boy Butch Casady.

Franny straightens at my side, not too blitzed to miss the meaning behind Tina's words.

"Tina, we were just leaving," I say, holding Franny's hand.

Sneering, the woman looking like a wolf in her fake fur coat, saunters forward, her hands sliding up my chest. "Butchy, come on. I thought we would have a little fun."

I grab her hand before she makes it far, removing it from my body. It's been almost two years since I've taken Tina home. Once I realized she was sleeping with anybody in town with a dick willing to use it, I haven't been back.

"Not a chance, Tina."

Jerking her hand from my grip, she's seething in anger. "When you get tired of offering handouts to the destitute," her eyes rake over Francine, "You know where to find me. After all, you never can stay away from me for too long, baby." I don't know what game she's playing, but it's ending now.

"I've managed to stay away from you just fine. Unfortunately, from what I've heard, Mark McDonald wasn't so lucky."

Rumor has it Mark was messing around with Tina and wound up with a nasty case of warts around his nuts. Unfortunately, they couldn't have been from his wife seeing as how she'd been out of town for months taking care of her ailing mother. So now he's dealing with warts and a divorce.

And what happens next is so fast, it takes me a beat to catch up.

Tina's face has turned wild, and her hand is raised, right in front of my face. Francine's holding onto her wrist, having stopped her from slapping me in midair.

"It really is uncouth for a woman to act such a way in public," she says releasing Tina's hand with a slight push.

I grab Franny's hand back into mine and head out the door when she says nonchalantly over her shoulder to Tina, "And that shade of lipstick is for loose women and hookers."

ELEVEN
DAMN RIGHT

This woman is full of fucking surprises.

Walking back towards my truck, I'm breathing heavily and my adrenaline is pumping. Not from what Tina said or did, but by the way Francine responded. I've never had a woman stand up for me like that before. And my dick appreciates the gesture greatly.

We are nearly to the truck, and I'm admittedly walking fast in order to get her in the cab and hopefully on my lap, when she stops fast, pulling back on her hands.

"Wait! Butch, stop!"

Crossing her arms and jutting out her hip, she plants her feet on the ground. "I am not getting in that truck with you until we talk about this."

"Talk about what, exactly?" I ask darkly. Thinking that I don't necessarily have to be in the cab in order to make out with her. I could probably make right here work just fine.

She throws her arm out to the side in the direction of the bar, "Her! You!" Raising her hand between us, motioning back and forth from our bodies, "Us!"

"I don't want to talk about her," I growl, reaching for her hand again. Not sure why she's angry at me.

She whips it back out of my reach. "Well, too bad. Because it seems I can't go out in this town without running into her. And *clearly* you guys were a thing. And even *more* clearly, she's not over it." Crossing her arms in front of herself, she asks, "What I need to know is, are *you* over it? Because, if you're not, then I need to know now."

Tilting my head, I collect my thoughts a minute before proceeding. It's obvious the alcohol is giving my normally shy and reserved girl a dose of liquid courage.

I start talking to her before I start walking to her. "Last I checked, I've got a spare bedroom full of pink and purple kid shit." I take a step. "My bathroom's got a basket full of makeup on the counter." Another step. "My shower has more shampoo, conditioner, and soap bottles sittin' in it than I could use in a year." One last step. "And I haven't slept in my own bed for almost a week." Whispering now, I grasp her head in my palm, running my fingers under her hair in the back. "What *I* need to know is, what part of all that makes you question whether or not I'm over it?"

"I'm not like her," Franny whispers back. "I'm not as strong or as confident."

I growl. "Bullshit." Gripping her face tighter, "Girls like that are a dime a dozen. But you? You're unlike anyone I've ever known. I don't fucking want anything but you, Franny."

Looking into each other's eyes, I need to know. "What do you want, Franny?"

"I don't know." She whispers back, tears in her eyes. "I want...I don't know." Her voice is starting to sound panicked.

"Don't do that, Franny." I say through my teeth. Our noses are almost touching. I ask again, "What - Do - You - Want?"

What she says next nearly brings me to my knees. I feel a wave of relief, satisfaction, and desire all bundled up into one fucking happy package.

"I want you, Butch." She whispers with her lips brushing against mine.

"Damn right." All of the pent-up emotion and sexual frustration come out in my kiss. Searing and not as gentle as I should be, I lose myself in her mouth.

She bites my bottom lip, gasping, "Take me home, Butch."

"Absolutely," I answer. Dragging her the few steps to the truck and opening the door for her. Once I'm in my seat, I've got the truck in gear and I'm pulling out of the parking lot with Francine under my arm. Not wasting any time to get us home.

She's kissing my neck, her hand caressing my chest. Licking and kissing her way up to my ear, she whispers, "I love how you smell." Her tongue flicks out across my lobe and I groan.

"Darlin', you keep that shit up and we're not making it to a bed."

Her giggle makes my dick twitch and as if she knew it, her hand slides down my chest, over my stomach, and right on top of my hard cock.

I grit my teeth as she rubs up and down over my jeans and I concentrate on not crashing the truck, trying to see through the explosion of stars in my eyes from what her hand is doing on my groin. "Franny, I'm not lying. You're killing me. A man only has so much control."

"I love that I can make you crazy," She whispers against my cheek.

Pulling onto my street, I need to make sure she understands what exactly is about to happen. "Sweetheart, listen to me." She's kissing down my neck again and I roughly take in a breath.

"Franny, I need you to hear me."

"Hmm?" She moans, her lips vibrate on my throat.

I pull into the driveway and throw the truck in park. Capturing her face in my hands, I give her one long, hard kiss. Keeping my nose pressed to hers, I lay it out. "You've been drinking and I've never been one to take advantage of a woman, Franny. But if you want this, if you want me, once we go inside - what happens between us tonight - there's no going back. Because once you're mine, Franny. *You're mine.* Do you get me?"

"Yes, Butch."

"I need to hear you say it. I need to hear you say you understand."

Her hands glide up my arms and clasp around my hands that are still holding her head. Pressing her forehead to mine, she sighs, "I'm yours."

That's the extent of my control. I hop out of the truck and jog around the front. Franny's already out and I slam her door and pick her up, throwing her over my shoulder.

She squeals out in laughter, holding onto the waist of my pants as I race to the backdoor. Kicking it closed behind me, I don't bother with lights, stalking through the house and up the stairs, not stopping until I'm in the bedroom and my legs hit the side of the bed.

Flipping her off my shoulder and onto the mattress, Franny lands on her back with a gasp. Her curly hair is wild on her head from being carried upside down and she's lying back on her elbows, looking up at me in anticipation.

Her bedroom eyes are following me. I shrug off my bomber jacket, letting it fall to the floor behind me. Franny starts rubbing her legs together, her pantyhose shimmering in the streetlamp light reflecting through the window.

Reaching back slowly, I grip the neckline of my shirt behind my head and pull it off, tossing it to the side.

My fingers are on my button when Franny sits up and crawls across the bed to where I'm standing like a wildcat. Her back arched in and her movements fucking feline.

Rising up on her knees, she grabs the front of my jeans and scooches forward until she's right in front of me.

Kissing my bare chest, Franny unbuttons my Levi's and pulls the zipper. Letting her take the reins, I bunch her hair in my hand to see her work.

Pushing my pants and boxers off at once, she slides my jeans down my thighs, her body lowering along with her soft hands. My cock springs free from its confinement and Franny takes me in her small, cool hand. Her fingers grip tight and run up and down the length of me.

"Fuck." I rumble, throwing my head back in delirium.

And because my head is back, because my eyes are squeezed closed thinking that having her hands on me was the definition of heaven, I don't know she's about to lick me. So, when her warm, wet tongue laps the tip of my dick, I hiss and pull my head forward.

Grabbing the base of my shaft, I yank Francine's head back and demand, "Suck it, sweetheart." Pointing my cock right at her lips.

Her hands grab my thighs, her eyes look up at me from where she's crouched on the bed, and she opens her mouth, taking me all in.

The slurping sound is fucking hot, but when I press her head in and she gags a little on my dick? Holy fuck, I almost spill it right inside her mouth.

Bending over, I pull Franny's dress up her back. She straightens up and I peel it off, letting it pool onto the floor at my feet. Our lips clash and she moans into my mouth. Tilting my head, my teeth scrape across hers and I suck her tongue.

I caress her neck, slowly stroking over her collarbone and down to her chest. Squeezing the soft mounds covered in white lace, I stop what I'm doing and step back to get a better look. "Is this the set from the store?"

"Mhm," She purrs, her hands gliding up her neck, pulling her hair on top of her head.

Taking in the white lace, I notice her hose are thigh highs, sheer with a matching white lace trim along the top to match her lingerie. Jesus. If I knew this was under that dress, we never would have left the house.

"You are breathtaking, Franny." I tell her, appreciating the beautiful woman on my bed.

Moving backwards, she shifts herself further up so that her head lands on one of the pillows. Opening her arms and her legs, she invites me to come to her.

Removing my blue jeans, the rest of the way, I kneel onto

the bed and crawl over her. I pull her tiny panties off and unclasp her bra from between her breasts. Not overly large, they fit in the palm of my hand and her nipples pebble and peak under my tweaking and twisting.

Her legs are writhing under me and I lower down, placing a kiss on the edge of her thigh highs. Continuing my journey across her center, my lips graze the soft mound of hair and I hear Franny gasp, grabbing my hair in anticipation. Just what I always knew. She smells like her own brand of candy.

"Can I kiss you here, Franny?" I ask, my words blowing across her pussy.

"Yes!" She cries out.

My first taste is a full lick from the core to the tip of her wet folds. Tangy and sweet, I growl and gorge on her velvet flesh.

Slowly, my finger slides inside of her, pumping into her entrance while sucking the tender nub in her folds. I've got a perfect view of her bobbing breasts and open mouth as I'm feasting.

I flick my tongue relentlessly in her creases, her sticky excitement coating my chin. I can feel her body shudder and her breath hitch right before her stomach heaves and she screams out my name in her release.

I bend down and grab my pants, pulling out a condom from my back pocket and throwing the jeans back down. I tear the wrapper open with my mouth, roll the rubber on, and climb onto the bed.

Moving on top of her, I balance on one arm. With my hand splayed next to her shoulder, I guide my dick into her pussy.

We both sigh in pleasure when my rim pushes into her opening.

Kissing the side of her head, I enter gently until I'm balls deep between her legs. Holding myself still, I'm braced on my shaking arms to give her body time to adjust to my intrusion.

Painstakingly steadily, I pull out almost all the way and slide in in one smooth, slick delve. "Two years," I murmur into her ear; my mind currently controlled by my dick.

"What?" She breathes back.

Rocking back and thrusting forward, she gasps and I groan. "For two years I dreamed what it would be like to be right here." Enforcing my meaning by swiveling my hips. Starting a steady rhythm of strokes, "For two years I wanted to be the guy that got to take you to bed."

With my admission, along with the gratification that it's finally my cock in her pussy, my plunges grow heavier and harder.

Holding her head in place with my arms caging her in, I ram ruthlessly into her. Her own arms are intertwined with mine and her slim legs wrapped around me as my body claims hers.

Francine's panting grows more ragged and when she climaxes again, squeaking in a silent cry, her body squeezing and tightening around my shaft, I curse and spill my seed inside of her. Her crotch milks me dry until I'm shuddering over her.

Moving to the side so that I don't crush her, I pull her to me and lightly rub her arm, her side and her leg. Wanting to touch her, still be a part of her.

Our breathing begins to stabilize and I kiss her shoulder, at the same time I reach down and pull off the used condom. Throwing it onto the floor like a fucking college preppy, my eyes are growing heavy and I don't want to get up. It's been a while since I've been comfortable in my bed and it feels pretty damn good to have her in my arms while doing it.

I'm nearly asleep, her fingers brushing whisper soft against my arm, when I hear her say into the quiet darkness, "I thought of you, too."

"Hm?" I ask, my eyes closed and my brain trying to sign off for the night.

She turns towards me and says, "I thought of you. For two years. And I - I came back here. I had nowhere else to go and I was hoping - hoping I'd fit in here and that maybe - maybe I'd find you, again. Is that crazy?"

I look down at her face, the sweat glistening on her brows. Every Goddamn time I'm sure she's shocked me for the last time, she goes and does it again. And it would be a lie if I said it doesn't do my ego good to know it wasn't just me thinking about a stranger from Quick Mart.

She's waiting for me to say something, and to be honest, I'm speechless. So, I kiss her instead. Making sure to show her exactly what she means to me. Our lips dance until we both break away, depleted and sated. We fall asleep holding one another.

TWELVE
This Woman Is Perfect

Francine wakes up first, pulling me from my sleep in the most spectacular way.

I can't say I've ever been woken up by a beautiful woman sucking my dick, but I *can* say that, now that I've experienced it, it's a helluva lot better than an alarm clock. Even if it is still the middle of the night.

Not wanting to miss a thing, I hold her hair back so I can see her go down on me. She's licking and sucking my cock like a damn popsicle, moaning around my dick. I groan when her pink tongue rims around my tip.

About to cum in her mouth, I pull her up by her arms. I want to flip positions on the bed putting me on top, so I grab her ass and start to roll over with her. She stops me, putting her hand on my chest and says, "My turn." She pushes my back to the mattress, straddling me.

"Yes, ma'am."

"Where's the condom?" She asks, kissing all over my face.

Jesus. Just smelling her, feeling her body touching mine makes me wild. "In the nightstand, top drawer."

Reaching over me to get to the table, her breast is perfectly poised in my face. I lift my head and I suck her tit, kneading the soft flesh.

Francine gasps, dropping the condom onto the bed so she can grab my head and push me harder against her nipple. I release her peak with a popping sound and she leans the opposite way, keeping her hand in my hair and pressing her other breast into my mouth. I grunt my approval and shower her needy nipple with attention.

Once both breasts are red and swollen, she tears open the condom and I follow her every move as she rolls it down my throbbing dick.

Francine bends forward and kisses my chest, my throat, my mouth. Alternating between pursed lip kisses and wet licks. She gives me a heavy, sensual kiss and bites my bottom lip before she sits straight up.

With a sly smile, she reaches behind her to find my hard, pulsing cock. Two fingers are on my shaft and the other ones are brushing against my balls.

Francine raises on her knees and pushes my rod forward. I lift my hips to help her guide it inside of her. Holding onto her legs while she seats herself fully, I growl at the wet heat consuming my dick and curling my toes.

"Oh my God," she exclaims, throwing her head back at the pressure.

Sitting stationary on top of me, she straightens her head and sucks her teeth. Caressing my stomach with her palms while her body adjusts to my hard dick.

Moving slowly, she gyrates against me, her body undulating over me like a wave. Rocking back and forth setting her own pace. With her hands on my pecs to hold her body up, I lay back, deciding to let her use me. Gliding my fingers up her thighs, down her thighs, over her legs and back up again, Franny rides me like a bull in slow motion.

Her breathing grows more ragged, her eyes squeeze shut, and I feel the quiver start in her legs and have a front seat view as it works its way up her body. Taking hold and causing her entire body to quake and convulse in explosion, tightening around my cock like a vise.

"Fuck!" I bellow, on the cusp of my own orgasm. I grab her ass cheeks and lift her up to make enough room for me to pound into her from underneath.

Off balance, Francine reaches out and grabs the wooden headboard for support, moaning low and long. With my feet pushing into the bed and my legs cocked up, I hammer into Francine until I shatter underneath her. Emptying myself in pulsating quakes of pleasure.

Still seeing stars, I hear Fanny pant, "God! That was amazing," Her breathing out of sorts.

I smirk, feeling pretty damn cocky, and smack her ass.

"Butch!" She yells out, laughing when I flip her onto her back. My half limp dick slips out of her pussy. My legs lay across hers, and I reach down to pull off the condom. Sliding my hand against the wet skin and hair from her cream, "God damn. You get so fucking wet for me."

Her eyes grow hooded and her fingers play in my chest hair. "It's never been like this before. I mean, for me."

"Darlin', just so we're clear, it's never been like this for me before, either."

Those doe eyes get big and she looks as if she doesn't believe me.

"I'll never lie to you, Franny. I won't cheat and I won't lie.

I may be an asshole sometimes, and I'm going to screw up on occasion, but I will never treat you bad."

Content with the trust I see on her face, I kiss her quickly and get out of bed. "I'll be right back, I've gotta clean up."

Scooping up the condom on the floor, I walk to the bathroom and throw the rubbers in the trash can. I'm about to piss when I hear the shattering of glass downstairs. "What the fuck?"

Running out of the bathroom and into the hallway, Francine is already in the bedroom doorway. "Stay here!" I tell her, taking three steps at a time down.

A quick look to my right shows me the living room is quiet. I skirt to my left and find the front window shattered, a brick on the floor, and cold winter wind blowing through the curtains. Rushing in, careful of the sharp shards, I hear her shrieks before I look through the fractured glass. Tina is standing outside, barefoot in the snow and drunkenly pacing across my front lawn.

"Come out you little bitch!"

Jesus. She has absolutely lost her mind. I bound upstairs in three steps and storm into the bedroom. Francine is wrapped in the sheet, staring out the window at Tina.

Pushing my leg into my jeans, I tell her, "I'll be back. Just stay up here, yeah?"

"Okay," she whispers, not looking at me.

Shoving my other leg through my pants, I walk over to where she's standing. "Franny," I pull her chin so her eyes meet mine. "I'll handle this and be back."

She nods and I kiss her forehead. I bend down and pick up my shirt, putting it on as I fly back down the steps.

Unlocking the front door, I stride out. "What the fuck, Tina? What the hell is wrong with you?"

"You're not just taking in girls right off the streets, but you're fighting their battles too?" She screams at me, taking a few steps back. Her fur coat from earlier is not on her body, her hair is standing on end, and in the streetlamp light, she looks absolutely unhinged.

"You just threw a brick through *my* window. So, yeah, this is my problem."

She closes the distance between us and pushes my shoulder. "I've got a *problem* with your whore. And I'll take it up with your whore!"

I grab Tina's upper arms, "You don't ever talk to her. You don't look at her. And you will never touch her." She pulls away from me and stumbles back.

I turn my back on her to go inside. She's already taken up too much time out of my evening.

"Are you threatening me Butch Casady?"

Not even bothering to turn back around, I tell her, "Hell yes, I am. If you ever come on my property again, I'll call Jax and have him haul your ass to the slammer."

Closing the door, I can still hear her screaming through the broken window.

"You've always been a loser!" Grabbing her hair at the side of her head, she laughs insanely, "God! I should have known better than to think you'd ever be anything more than a dirty greaser!"

I wait for the sound of an engine and pull the curtains closed in the dining room. Taking a deep breath, I pocket my hands and shake my head. What the fuck did I ever see in her? She wasn't even a good lay. Not compared to what I had tonight, that's for damn sure. Tonight with Franny was - fuck, it was the shit you see in movies.

"Well, I get it now."

Not realizing Francine was in the kitchen, I pitch my neck to the side but keep my eyes down to the ground. Not ready yet to face her after what just happened.

"What's that?" I ask, spinning my head forward to look through the sliver of opening in the curtains. For the first time in my life, I find myself embarrassed about my life. About my past decisions. I've never been one to give a damn what other people thought of me. It's unnerving to realize that someone's opinion actually matters that much.

Coming up behind me, Francine slides her hands under my tented arms and wraps her own around my waist, folding her hands together on my stomach. Resting her head against my back, she says, "I get why you were looking for me." Blowing out a breath, she continues, "It's the same reason I was looking for you, I guess."

"Yeah? And why's that you think?" I ask her quietly.

"Because we both knew we were with the wrong people." Francine kisses my back, right between my shoulder blades.

I squeeze my eyes tight and lean my head back to rest on top of hers. "Fuck, Franny. It feels good to hear you say that."

My mind begins going through what all I'll need from the garage to fix the window. I better get on it before the house gets too cold.

"I'm sorry she ruined our night."

"Oh, she didn't ruin my night. I'm not sure that would even be possible." Squeezing her arms tight around my waist, she says, "Did I already tell you how amazing you are in bed?"

Despite the circumstances, I laugh and turn around to hold her. "Darlin', I'm not sure if you know this, but that's not something you can ever tell a man too much."

Giggling, she pushes up on her toes and meets my kiss. Running my hands up her arms, I feel the goosebumps on her skin from the winter air blowing through the curtains. Breaking our kiss, I see she's in one of my t-shirts and rub my hands over her ass. "I love it when you wear my shit."

"Well, we could have spent a lot less at Montgomery Wards if I'd have known you just wanted me in your old clothes."

Smacking her ass playfully, I push her towards the steps. "I've got to board this window and clean up a bit. Go upstairs and keep the bed warm for me, yeah?"

"Yeah," she whispers. Coming back to kiss me one more time, she says against my lips, "I get cold at night. I hope you like to cuddle."

God damn. This woman is perfect. "Sweetheart, any activity that involves you and your body, I can guaran-damn-tee I will like." Squeezing her ass one last time I tell her, "Now get upstairs."

By the time I get the window covered, the glass cleaned up and the room vacuumed- I did it three extra times because I was worried about Lou Lou stepping through small glass shards- I climb into bed exhausted.

Francine's hair is fanned out around her head all over the pillow and she's snoring. It's a low, cute sound that reminds me of Granny's cat.

Smiling, I pull her over to me and tuck her under my arm. Throwing her leg over mine and her arm across my middle, she contentedly sighs in her sleep.

Yep. I can definitely get used to this. Closing my eyes, my last thought is that I need to measure the window before I head into work tomorrow so I can order the replacement.

THIRTEEN
IT'S THE LITTLE THINGS

The next few weeks with Francine and Lucy Lou are pretty damn good.

We have all fallen into our new routines and to be honest, it feels like they've always been here. Or at the very least, as if they were missing when they weren't.

I start my day early, heading into the garage at 5 am. So, when I get home around 6, it's damn nice to walk into a clean house and dinner in the oven. I guess I never realized how much I hated coming home after a long day to a cold, dark house until I didn't have to.

Turns out, Francine can cook. I mean, the woman can *cook*. There hasn't been a single meal yet that wasn't good. And even though I never expected it, she takes care of shit around the house while I'm gone.

She keeps a tidy home, which is much appreciated, and I haven't had to wash a single sock for nearly a month, so that's fucking fabulous. To top it all off, she's been taking Lou Lou to story time at the library twice a week and even joined a Jazzercise group, though I told her countless times she didn't need to. She's made a few friends there and seems to enjoy it, which makes me happy, too.

We have a standing date night on Wednesdays at KJ's with the boys that Granny holds us to so she can get her time with Lou Lou. Which is funny considering she walks over and eats dinner with us nearly every damn night.

And the way my boys treat her, you'd think all four of us were dating Franny. And to her relief, I've stopped getting jealous - realizing that it's just that they all see, and appreciate, the woman she is.

There's a light in Francine's eyes that wasn't there before. She's easy to talk to, argues with me constantly, and laughs even more than that. And she has no problem with putting my guys in their place. Point is, she's really finding her way around Eddington. And I am really finding my way around her.

So, when I got the call from Jax this morning, who had received a region-wide fax from the Brownston police department concerning a stolen yellow Pacer, it put me in a really fucking bad mood.

Jax had already matched vin numbers to the jalopy sitting in the back of Wren's garage and no surprise - it matched.

"I have to let them know we have the car, Butch. I can put it off for a while, but I'll eventually have to call it in," Jax said over the phone.

"Damn," I grumble. Rubbing my eyes.

"Yeah, I feel you," Jax says. "Asshole doesn't look for his woman or kid, but puts out an APB on his shit car."

"They're *not* his," I bite back. "And I don't give a rat's ass about that car."

Jax laughs, not at all phased by my foul temper. "Were you ever going to tell Franny that it's fixed?"

I scowl. Wren finished working on it over two weeks ago, but Francine's been just fine- and a hell of a lot safer- borrowing Granny's car. So, I didn't see the importance of telling her. I figured it was something we'd deal with when it came back around.

"You tell me. Say you got a girl and a kid - you gonna let them ride around in a fucking Pacer?"

"Hell no," Jax answers.

"Exactly," I mutter. Then an idea hits me. "Listen, is there any way you can get the guy's information? Maybe we can skip all the damn legal steps and just give him what he wants straight."

Jax might have been originally voted in as Chief, and he may be serving his second term because no one else ran for the position, but there is no doubt to anyone in town that he's the best man for the job. He's good at what he does and he gets shit done.

"Yeah. Give me a few hours. You thinking of settin' up a little meet and greet?" He asks. It's not lost on me that this isn't exactly on the "up and up" for a Chief. But, Jax has been my pal for a long time and he'd do anything for me. And he knows I'd return the favor no questions asked.

"Somethin' like that," I answer. "I gotta go, buddy. Keep me posted."

Hanging up, I stare at the grease-stained phone for a minute. Things are good with me and Francine. I think she's happy and she hasn't brought up the subject of finding her own place again, so I'm assuming she's just as content with the way things are moving as I am.

I decide I'm not going to say anything to her. Not yet, at

least. There's no reason to get her worked up and upset over it.

And that's what I continually told myself the rest of the day whenever I thought about it. Which was pretty much all the fucking time.

It's almost time to head out when Jax finally gets back to me.

"I've got his info. Name's Stephen James Black - 25 - originally from Hilford. Dropped out of high school. Has a few minors on his record. Basically, he's a topnotch loser."

"No fucking surprise," I tell him.

"Butch, he's claiming she attacked him and took his car." Jax adds.

I don't answer. There's plenty I'm thinking, but nothing I want to fucking say at the moment.

"Now what?" Jax asks.

Grabbing the phone tight, I grit, "Now, I need you to set up a meeting with him and me. I think we can handle this without further assistance from the police department. You get me?"

"Yeah, I get you," Jax responds before ending the call.

Now, me and that punk have got a little date at a small trucker's cafe off the turnpike tomorrow afternoon. A few hours drive for me, a few hours in a cab for him. But it doesn't matter. I'd drive 24 fucking hours if it meant putting this all to rest.

On the way home, I remember Francine saying we were out of peanut butter and needed milk. I turn into the Quick Mart just before I pass the entrance, waving to one of Granny's card night friends leaving the parking lot in her

Buick.

Making a quick walk-through of the store, I grab everything we need as fast as I can. I'm more anxious than normal to get back home tonight due to all the unexpected happenings of the day. I add a few last-minute additions to the cart and check-out.

Throwing the bags into the bed of the truck, I start the Black Beauty and pull out onto Main Street. I grip the wheel tight and concentrate on trying to steady my breath and bench my anger. Francine will pick up on it as soon as she sees me, and I don't plan on filling her in on tomorrow's plans.

But, dammit. The fact that that fucker accused Francine of stealing that car. The fact that he thinks he's going to make up whatever story fits into whatever the Hell he's trying to get, makes my blood boil.

I pull into my driveway at the same time Granny's walking out her door with a diaper bag over her shoulder and Lou Lou in her arms. Franny must have gone out today.

Hopping out, I pocket my keys and jog over to meet her before she gets too far over.

"Woah! Stop right there, Gran. I got her." I tell her as I turn the corner and meet her on the front path, putting my hands out to take Lucy from her side.

As soon as Lucy sees me, she starts giggling. "Hey pretty girl," I coo.

Lou Lou throws herself out to me and I catch her, tossing her into the air. She squeals with delight and I catch her, bend my legs and do it again.

This is her favorite game to play with me. Well, this and

anything that has to do with me laying on the ground and her climbing on top of me.

"How was she?" I ask, gently taking the strap of the bag off Granny's shoulder and putting it onto mine.

"Perfect as always," Granny answered. "She does feel a little warm to me, though. She's probably cutting her molars." Her soft, wrinkled hand rubs through Lucy's tight curls. "Poor thing."

Immediately, I raise my hand and touch her forehead. It may be cold outside, but she definitely feels too warm. "I've got to get her inside, Gran. Thanks for watching her today." I say as I quickly lean down to kiss her.

Smiling, a twinkle in her eye, Granny cups my face in her hands. "It is the highlight of my day, Butch."

There is no doubt in my mind that that is the absolute truth.

"You coming out for dinner?" I ask, already knowing that whatever Francine's makin', she's makin' enough for everyone.

"No, not tonight. You enjoy your dinner with just the three of you."

Starting to walk back around the corner of the house, I tell her over my shoulder, "All right. But you know how she is. Expect some leftovers in a bit."

Francine will accept no for an answer in regards to whether or not Gran eats at the table with us, but she refuses not to feed her. In Francine's words, "Either here or there, you're eating what I make."

"Bye Bye ditty and danny!" Lucy Lou calls out, waving at Gran. In Lucy language, kitty is ditty, and granny is danny.

I hear Gran laughing as she walks back into the house, "Goodbye my love!".

Picking up the bags as I walk by the truck, I step onto the stoop and Lou Lou instantly sees Francine standing at the stove through the window of the door. "Mama!" She screams, clapping and giving her that toothy smile.

Francine's back is to us, but I can see she's wearing her bright pink and blue exercise clothes. Meaning she must have gone to her Jazzercise class today.

And if I'm being honest, I love it when she goes. She may not need to lose a single pound, seeing as how her body is fucking perfection already, but damn. Being able to fully enjoy the tights and leotard hugging her body are what my dreams are made of. And the high ponytail and sweat-band on top makes my dick even harder, if that's even possible.

Turning around from where she's just pulled out a casserole dish from the oven, Francine beams back and rushes to the door to open it for us.

"Hello!" She greets us, grabbing the bags from my hand.

I smell meatloaf and mashed potatoes and my stomach growls in response. "It smells good in here."

Francine spins around to place the groceries on the table. And just like that, my bad mood disappears.

There was a time that whenever I held Lou Lou, Francine would rush to get her out of my arms. Not because she didn't trust me, but because she was worried that me holding Lucy, playing with Lucy, doing literally fucking *anything* with Lucy, was putting me out.

And with a little patience and a lot of reiterating the fact that there was nothing taxing about carrying around the curly haired little girl that has given me more hugs and kisses in the time I've known her than I've ever received in my life, Francine finally figured it out. I don't just come home to my woman. I come home to my girls.

So, Franny choosing to take the groceries from me, and not Lucy, means the fucking world.

It may be cliche as Hell, but it's true. It's the little things. The little things mean the most. The little things thaw the cold and warm the heart. And my Franny? She's fucking full of the little things.

She pulls out both jars of peanut butter and sets them on the table. One jar of creamy for me and Lucy and one jar of chunky for Francine.

"You got Lucky Charms?" Francine asks excitedly when she sees the box.

I grunt, "I don't know why you like that shit. But yeah, I got you some."

"What are these for?" Francine asks again, pulling out the bouquet of red carnations.

"Sweetheart, if a man brings you flowers and you gotta ask what they're for, then the man's not doin' his job right."

Smiling from ear to ear, she practically puts her entire face into the opening of the flowers. I hear her take a deep sniff. "They smell *so* good."

"Not as good as you," I tell her as I'm kicking off my boots.

"Thank you, Butch." She says, slinking up to me in her sexy way, with her sexy clothes. She rises on her toes and gives me a kiss that shows just how thankful she is.

"Mmm," I mumble against her lips, my free hand finding its way around to her perky ass. "I need to bring home flowers more often."

Slapping my arm, still smiling huge, she opens the cabinet and pulls down a big mason jar. Turning on the faucet, she starts filling it up for the flowers.

"Granny thinks this girl has the start of a fever." I tell Francine as I pull off Lucy Lou's shiny and puffy pink winter coat.

"What?" Francine asks, whirling around with concern on her face. Lou Lou starts to fuss when she's pulled from my arms and Francine dances with her, shushing and kissing her cheeks and head. "She does feel warm," She says against Lucy's skin.

Taking my own coat off, I throw it over the back of a chair.

"I'll grab the thermometer from upstairs," I tell her, stopping to kiss Francine's cheek on my way past.

I run up the steps, grab the thermometer from the bathroom, and run back down, hearing Lucy fuss the whole time.

"Did Jean say if she was fussy?" Francine asks as she pulls Lou Lou's arm through the purple sleeve of her shirt.

"Nope. Said she was perfect." I answer. "She wouldn't ever tell us anything else, anyway."

Seeing Francine struggle to get the thermometer under a growingly irritated Lou Lou's arm, I pull the little one into my embrace. She instantly settles against my chest and allows her Mama to lift up her little wrist and place the stick in her armpit.

I rock gently and rub Lucy's back while we both hold her, waiting for the beep.

Francine and I are staring at one another. Lucy Lou between us. And I can't help myself from asking, "Are you happy Franny?"

She looks surprised at my question. But then a warm smile spreads across her face and she leans farther into our little group huddle. "I am so happy, Butch."

"Good." I answer. Feeling a relief of tension in my chest I hadn't realized was there.

The beeping sounds and we both look down to the small screen of the thermometer.

"99 degrees," says Francine.

"Gran said she's probably just cutting molars," I console her.

Nodding, she pulls away from us. "I think we should give her Tylenol and some juice before we eat."

"Sure thing," I say, my lips in the riot of curly hair.

Once she's taken the medicine and drank the juice, we try to sit down for a sort-of-warm meal. But Lou Lou wants nothing to do with sitting in her seat. And she's not thrilled about being on Francine's lap.

"Let me try," I tell Francine, wiping my mouth with my napkin. Just like before, as soon as her little head hits my chest, she snuggles down. Thankfully, I didn't work on anything too greasy at work today so my t-shirt's mostly clean.

"I guess we know who she prefers," Francine smirks, finally getting to take a bite of her meatloaf.

I wink at her. "Do you blame her?"

Scoffing, she says, "You're ridiculous."

"Darlin', you know I'm a magnet for the ladies."

Her mouth opens before she says through her laughter, "You did not just say that!"

"Proof's right in front of you, sweetheart." I smirk like a

cocky ass, rubbing Lucy's back. "I've got more women than most men."

"Oh, really? And exactly how many women do you have?" Her voice sounds a little hesitant.

"Two. You...her...here in my house."

"That we are, Butch. Me and her...in your house." Francine answers quietly, placing her hand on top of the one I have resting on Lucy's back. She's got those bedroom eyes that I've begun to recognize and my cock jumps in acknowledgment.

"You got me red carnations," she adds.

"I did."

"Do you remember?" Her voice is a mere whisper.

"I remember, Franny." I tell her just as softly back.

I can see the tears forming in her eyes and I groan at the sight. "Don't do that." I say, still holding Lucy with one hand and cupping her chin with my other.

"That night," she breathes deeply. "That night, when I first met you, when you helped me - when you - when you gave me those flowers." Her head nods to the jar of flowers in the middle of the table. "You really did give me the strength I needed."

"Darlin', I hate to break it to you and ruin any ideas you may have of me bein' your hero, but you were already strong. The flowers just boosted your confidence a bit."

"They did." She agreed and her eyes lit up. "And they lasted for weeks! It's true, carnations really are -"

"Survivors," I finish her sentence for her. Remembering every word from that night in the Quick Mart two years ago. "And so are you," I tell her, squeezing her chin before letting it go.

"Now eat. I have a feeling we're in for a long night with this one," starting back rubs on the sleeping girl in my arms again.

Fourteen
Chocolate

Last night was a long one, but not all bad.

Almost as soon as we had finished eating dinner, Lucy Lou woke up fevered and grouchy.

Francine tried everything to get her to settle down the remainder of the night. Gave her a bath, a cup of juice, warm milk, her favorite toys... nothing worked.

After giving her the next dose of Tylenol, Francine sent me to bed for the night. Telling me that at least one of us should get some rest.

And I did sleep. But it was restless and only for a few hours.

Every time I woke up to toss and turn, Lucy Lou's crying seemed to get louder.

Finally feeling like a world-class dick for laying upstairs and not helping, I got my ass up and went downstairs.

Walking into the family room, the lights were off and I saw an exhausted Francine rocking a screaming Lou Lou on the Lazyboy recliner.

Startled at my presence, Francine looked worried. "I'm so sorry we woke you up! I've tried everything to get her to stop -"

"Don't apologize, Franny. I just came down to see if I could help." I told her, reaching my arms out to take Lucy from her.

"She's just miserable." Francine says over the crying.

As soon as I have her in my arms, her shrill screams quiet. And right after her little head hits my chest, she's sound asleep. Clearly spent from hours of fussing.

"Thank God," Francine whispers, falling back into the chair with her eyes closed.

"Let's switch. You head up and get a few z's and I'll stay down here with her."

"Are you sure?" She asks, the bags under her eyes a dead giveaway to how much she's going to fight me on this.

"Yep." I tell her, settling myself in on the couch.

And on the couch is where we stay for almost four hours. Lucy's woken up a few times throughout, moving her head or wrapping her arm around my neck as if she's checking to make sure I'm still there.

My back was protesting and after feeling her head with my cheek, it seemed her fever had finally broken. So, I decided to try to put her upstairs in her bed.

I tiptoed through the house carrying Lucy like I was in a minefield. And who the Hell knew that the wood steps creaked and groaned so much when you walked on them?

By the time I made it to the spare room and laid her down painstakingly slowly on the little mattress, my pits were sweaty from the effort of not waking her up.

Once I was sure she was asleep, I stealthily left the room and closed the door. Making sure to not release the door knob until it was fully in place. Who knew I was a freaking silent ninja? Those weird ass turtles got nothing on me.

Taking a deep breath of relief, I quietly walk into my bedroom and try not to rouse Francine.

Just getting comfortable, I pull the blanket over me when she scooches close, her front to my back. Resting her arm around my middle, she whispers, "I owe you."

I chuckle. "I take many forms of payment. But my favorite doesn't have a damn thing to do with paper."

"Hmm," She mumbles against my back. "An equal opportunity payment. I like it." Her cool hand glides down my stomach and her fingers slide under the waistband of my underwear.

Palming my dick, growing harder with each pass of her hand, Francine kisses me between my shoulder blades. "I feel so safe with you."

There are a million things she could have said to turn me on, but her saying that? When she's laying in my bed, in my house, with Lucy Lou sound asleep the next room over? *Nothing* could trump the way her words made me feel.

Growling my approval, I turned over and smashed my lips to hers while I pushed her down into the pillow. Slanting my head to get my tongue deeper, I wedged my hand behind her and pulled her forward. Grabbing the hem of her soft nightshirt, I dragged the silk up and over her body, tossing it onto the floor.

"On your knees," I told her, pushing myself up.

She complied immediately and I stood to remove my boxers and grab a condom from the drawer. Tearing the package open with my teeth, I rolled on the rubber and climbed back on the bed.

Crouching on all fours with her ass in the air and her head resting on her hands, I stop for a beat to appreciate the view. "Look at you," I whisper in awe, rubbing her ass and thighs, my rough, callused hands catching on the black lace of her panties.

Looping my fingers into the side of the lace, I pulled them down to her upper thighs and kneel down behind her to taste her.

My tongue has a mind of its own when it comes to Francine's pussy. Using my fingers to separate her wet folds, I licked and sucked mercilessly while listening to the mewls and moans vibrating through her body.

"Butch, Oh My God!" She loudly whispered, burying her head into the mattress to muffle the sound.

I could feel her climax shake the bed and I happily lapped up the extra nectar coating her pussy from her excitement.

Not able to wait any longer, we both rose up on our knees. "Spread your legs sweetheart," I told her as I guided my dick to her entrance. And with one full, hard push, we were connected.

She lets out a shocked intake of air as her body flails forward, my attached body following, caging her in.

I kiss her shoulder before pushing up and raise myself fully behind her.

When I grab her hips, a primal almost animalistic compulsion takes over me. Grasping a handful of Francine's hair with one hand, holding tight to her hip with the other I pounded into her.

Maybe it was the pissed off overthought of the upcoming meeting with her dickhead ex, or maybe it was what she just said to me, but I was overcome with the urge to claim her.

The room was quiet except for our heavy breaths and the quick, wet slapping of our bodies meeting in union.

Looking at her upturned face and my grasp on her hair are the only things holding me to that moment and not losing myself in my drive to possess her.

I hear the small, squeaking sound she makes before she climaxes and rear my body over hers once more, my chest slamming against her back. Keeping the same rhythm with my cock, I put all my weight on one arm and cover her mouth with the other right before she explodes in pleasure, yelling into my palm.

Her pussy clamped around my dick, I felt the aftermath of her orgasm still rippling and surging the warm velvet surrounding me and my balls tightened. "Fuck."

Removing my hand from her mouth, I wrap both around her neck. Pulling us both upright to our knees, I use my grip on her to piston her up and down on my groin until my own release takes over.

Burying my face into the skin of her neck, I groan my satisfaction and squeeze her throat tightly, pushing her body down to take all of me.

We both passed out in depleted exhaustion and didn't wake again until we heard the sound of babbling and cooing coming from the room next door.

Realizing I had slept in, and had a shit ton of shit to do at work before my meeting with the dickhead, I showered, dressed, and ate in a hurry.

I told Francine I'd be home late, probably just in time to pick her up and head to KJ's for wings, and I kissed my girls on the way out the door.

Lou Lou stuffing a handful of cheerios into her mouth and Franny sipping on her second cup of joe - both of them were smiling and happy as I walked out, even though we're all tired as Hell. Lucy's fever broke sometime in the night and she was back to normal (thank Christ). If I thought I was a softie when it came to women crying, I'm a total cream puff when it comes to the tears of little girls.

Now here I am, smushed in the driver's seat of the piss-yellow box of metal. Cramped inside for over two hours just to return it to the fucker that doesn't even deserve this hunk of junk.

Following Jax's cruiser, we take the exit off the turnpike and cross straight over the intersection into the parking lot of Trucker's Cafe.

Jax is in uniform and the looks we're getting walking into the joint leads me to believe there's a whole lot of not good shit going on around here.

"You know what this kid looks like?" Jax asks me as we walk in the door, conversations and dishes clanking covering the sound of country music coming through the ceiling speakers.

"Yep." The tension must be evident in my voice.

"Try to use your words and not your fists," Jax warns me.

I spot the weasel sitting in a booth in the corner, smoking a cigarette. His blonde hair looks about the same except the rat tail in the back. That's new. And fucking ridiculous.

He's wearing a sleeveless Bulls jersey in the dead of winter and because he's sprawled out in the bench seat like a punk, I see one of his sissy-assed pegged pant legs sticking out from the table, jumping in nervousness.

"You've got to be kidding me," Jax mutters under his breath. "Our Franny was with that?"

I only grunt in response and walk to the back of the restaurant.

Taking a seat at the counter right across from the booth, Jax makes eye contact with him before settling in his stool.

I slide into the opposite booth, making sure my eyes show the instability of anger I feel being so near to him.

Confusion takes over his face when it's me and not the chief of police that sits across from him. His eyes darting from Jax's back to me.

When Jax called him up yesterday, it was to inform him that the banana car had been found. This meeting was supposedly to hand over the vehicle and fill out the theft report.

"Who the fuck are you?" He asks, sitting up in his seat.

Folding my hands in front of me, my black leather jacket creaks in the movement. "Name's Butch."

He laughs, like my name is some joke. "Well, *Butch*, I don't know what the fuck is going on, but you're sitting at the wrong table bucco."

"Nah, *Stevie*, I'm at the right table." I reach into my pocket and pull out the keys to the Pacer. Keeping them in my fist, I slam my hand on the table and Stephen jumps.

Smiling, I slide the keys across the table, telling him, "Here's how this'll go, *bucco*. You're gonna take these keys, take your piece of shit car, and drop the theft report."

Leaving my hand covering the keys right in front of the asshole, I raise my brow, waiting for his response.

Looking from me to the keys and back again, he squints

his eyes. "Where'd you get the car?"

I don't answer and we just continue our fucking stare-off.

His eyes open wide and he laughs out loud. "You're fucking her, aren't you?" Laughing again even louder, "Jesus! Did she send you here?"

Shaking his head and sneering, "What a bitch. I fucking knew she wasn't worth the hassle."

I tighten my fingers around the keys and grit my teeth. Out of the corner of my eye, I see Jax sitting higher in his seat.

Smiling, he says, "I guess we're in a club now." Chuckling at his own joke. "I think we can both agree she's an easy lay."

That's it. Reaching over, I grab the fucker's jersey and pull him over the table so I can sit easy while laying it out. The plastic cup of soda tips over and spills into his lap while his wimp hands grip mine, trying to break my hold. I seethe, "Now, see, you had to go and make this hard. You and me? We're not friends. But I'm gonna do you a solid and give you a warning. You *ever* speak of Francine that way again, and you'll be fuckin' sorry."

Pulling him a smidge closer to me, I ask, "We clear?"

"Yes," he stutters right before I release his shirt and push him back into his seat.

The keys had fallen to the floor in our scuffle. Reaching out my leg, I put my boot over the keys and slide them across the floor. "You dropped these."

Bending down from his bench, he goes to pick them up but I don't lift up my boot. He looks up to me.

"Say please, Stevie."

His eyes are scathing, shooting darts at mine; he grits out, "*Please.*"

Slowly, I lift my foot from the floor, allowing him just enough space to pull the keys out. But not without him having to touch the bottom of my boot doing so.

I stand from my seat, tucking my hands into my pockets. Jax stands behind me.

Looking down at the soda-drenched jackass, I say my goodbyes. "I think we're on the same page. Francine is no longer your "hassle" and you're gonna take your little dick, tuck it into your little pussy car, and you and I can chalk this up as an unfortunate meeting."

Stephen's face turns red as he spits out, "And what about the kid? I think I deserve something for putting up with the brat for the past few years."

A rage I have never felt before in my life overtakes me. Jax puts his hand on my shoulder in an attempt to ground me and the asswipe sees it, reveling in the tone of my fury. Knowing damn well he's hit a chord.

Shrugging his shoulders, he takes a deep breath and blows it out. "You see, that's my kid. I guess you could say I feel a little attached to it."

I take the two steps between him and me, leaning down over the table with my face right the fuck in his. "Chocolate."

Laughing nervously as he looks up at me, he asks, "What?"

"The kid's favorite ice cream," I say. Followed by, "Two percent."

Thinking he's real funny, he mocks, "What's that? Your IQ?"

"It's the milk she drinks, you fuck face. Four hours is the total hours of sleep she got last night due to her fever. Cheerios are her favorite cereal. Five is the number she can count to without stumblin'. She's got her mother's blue eyes, her curls, and her personality. There isn't a lick of you in her, thank fuck. And she's not an "it" - her name's Lucy Lou."

Slamming my hand on the table, the pansy jumps once more and glances at the long envelope I pulled out of my pocket and am holding out to him. "Yeah. See, I kinda figured this was how it was gonna go."

Trying to pull the thick envelope from my hand, I resist a minute just to make him squirm. And when he's finally able to open it and see the bulk of cash stuffed inside, I watch his face calculating all the shit he can buy with the money.

"When you get back to Brownston, you're going to call the police department and tell them you were high when you lost your car." Confusion passes over his face, almost like he doesn't know what I'm talking about. "Say you found it at your drug-dealer's house for all I fucking care. And I never, *never*," encroaching down on him so hard he has to shrink down, "want to see your sorry ass ponytail ever again. If I do, I'm gonna let my fists do the talking. Get me?"

He sizes me up and then down, right to my Rolex. It hasn't escaped my notice that he's been eying it since I sat down. "Well, you paid me for the girl and kid. Now what are going to give me to stay away?"

I glare at him and he returns my stare with a smug smile, raising his brow in question.

Fucker.

I take off my grandfather's watch and put it down between us.

Taking one last chance to look him over from top to bottom, I push off the table and turn around to walk out.

Jax takes my place, leaning in over the jackass, "Take Eddington off your radar. You don't stop in my town, you don't drive my streets. If you do, I'll know it. And I'll personally help you find your way out."

Getting into the driver's seat of the cruiser, Jax says, "We heading home?"

"Yeah. Just need to stop at Wren's first," I answer, closing the passenger door.

FIFTEEN
FREE AND CLEAR

Francine was ready to go when I got home.

She had already taken Lou Lou to Gran's house and was waiting for me on the couch reading a book.

I kissed her hello, changed my clothes, and we left.

Walking into KJ's behind Franny, I take a beat to appreciate her tight ass in those Jordache jeans. Her loose pink sweatshirt is draping over her shoulder and her hair is falling loose around her.

Lynyrd Skynyrd's Free Bird is blasting throughout the room and we're greeted with the usual chorus of "Hey's!" and "Hiya's" from all the patrons.

Taking our normal seats at the bar, Kurt brings over a beer and Franny's white wine. He stocks it and keeps it cold, reserved just for her.

"Thanks Kurt," Franny says, a huge smile on her face.

"You're welcome, sweetheart," he tells her before looking at me. "How'd the day go?"

Seemingly an innocent question, he knows exactly what Jax and I were up to earlier. "Good."

"Get everything handled?" He asks, wiping the bar down, giving the impression we're just shooting the shit like we always do so as to not raise any alarms to Francine.

"Yep," I answer, taking a swig of Coors.

Swiveling her barstool around so her legs were between mine, Francine laughs as she wraps her arms around my neck. "My man of few words."

Kissing her, I pull my head back. "How was your day, darlin'?"

"Good! Ran to Montgomery Wards for some Spring dresses and shoes for Lou Lou. She's growing too fast!"

"Hm," I smile. "Did you find anything else good at the store?"

She gives me a sexy smile and leans forward, whispering, "Maybe. And maybe I'm wearing it right now, too."

Sliding my hand down her back, and then up her sweat-shirt, I feel the lace under my fingers. My body gets hot and I bury my head in her neck, taking a long inhale of her sweetness. "I say we skip the wings and go back home."

Giggling, she pushes against my chest. "Good things come to those who wait, Butchy."

I narrow my eyes on her. She loves to use that annoying nickname whenever she's giving me a hard time.

Her hand grasps my chin, and her lips form a dramatic pout, "Don't be a Grumpy Gus. You get me to yourself all night." Knowing damn well that it would take something big to get her to miss out on our Wednesday night with the boys.

Grabbing the back of her neck, "I should be raving jealous about how much you love my friends." My lips are so close to hers, that we kiss with every word I speak.

"It's not my fault you know how to pick 'em," she answers

against my mouth.

Pulling back, I look at her intently and rub her leg. "I sure do."

Her face warms and I'm about to kiss her again when a hand claps down on my shoulder.

I look up to a smirking Wren. "It's time lover boy," he says, winking at Francine.

"Time for what?" She asks, sitting up in her seat.

Taking one more swig of beer, I stand up and grab her hand. "Come on and I'll show you," I answer, pulling her to her feet and towards the door we just came in through.

Wren and Kurt follow us outside, the door closing out the sound of music and voices from inside.

And when Francine sees Jax leaning against a green car parked in front of the bar, his uniform still on and his arms crossed in front of him, smiling at her real big, she looks at me confused. "What in the world is going on?"

Jax stands up straight and throws a set of keys to me. I catch them with one hand and promptly turn to her, pull up the small hand I'm still holding, and place the keys in her palm.

"It's an AMC Eagle. A little used, but in great shape. Safe and reliable. The wagon will give you plenty of room for all of Lou Lou's shit." I tell her, watching her face go from confusion to understanding.

"You - you bought me a car?"

The lighting outside the bar isn't great, so I can't make out what her eyes are saying, but her voice is quiet and unsure.

"What about the Pacer?" She asks, looking from me to Wren.

Wren looks down at his feet, letting me take the lead. "Couldn't find all the parts he needed. Wren's just gonna junk it and sell it in pieces."

Her eyes narrow on mine. "I thought he ordered all the parts."

"Darlin', he wasn't able to get 'em all. Plus, this car is much better suited to the weather here in Eddington. And, it's got AC for summer."

Putting my hand on the side of her face, I add, trying to gauge what's going on in that pretty head, "Now you don't have to borrow Granny's car anytime you want to leave the house."

"But, where did it come from?" She asks me.

"Wren had it in the garage. I towed it a few months ago, dropped it off to him, and he fixed it. The owner never claimed it, so he filed a lien, got a clean title, and hadn't gotten around to selling it yet. So, I bought it off him. Wren cleaned it, Jax drove it here, and now it's yours. Free and clear," I explain.

"And now it's mine. Free and clear," she quietly repeats, squinting past me to the car. I can hear the uncertainty in her voice.

The boys are all looking at each other, not sure if this is going to go down as smooth and happy as we'd hoped.

A cry escapes her lips and my heart drops, reaching out to her to console her. I'm not sure why in the hell she's crying. But instead, she jumps into my arms and laughs. "Butch! Are you serious?"

Smashing her lips to mine, I can taste the warm saltwater of her tears. "Thank you!"

I set her down on her feet and her heels are barely on the asphalt before she's hugging Wren and kissing his cheek. "Thank you, Wren!"

Then jumping over to Jax and Kurt, doing the same damn thing.

"You boys sure know how to surprise a girl," she says through her tears and laughter.

Kurt lifts up an unopened bottle of champagne he has in his hands. "I know it's not a boat, but that thing's nearly as big as one." The boys laugh, and he says, cocking his chin to the wagon, "Thought you'd want to christen it."

Before she takes the bottle, Kurt wraps it tight in the towel he keeps over his shoulder. "This is all so crazy," she says through her giggles and walks to the front bumper of the jeweled tone car.

"You've got to name it first, Fran!" Kurt yells out.

She stands for a moment, staring at her car. Her bottom lip tucked into her teeth. Turning her head to me, the moisture in her eyes reflecting in the low light of the pub sign above us. "Lucky Charm," she answers quietly.

I nod my head and smile.

Francine breaks the wrapped bottle against the bumper, and the boys hoot and holler, clapping their hands. Wren picks her up and turns her around in the street as I stand on the sidewalk, my hands in my pockets, enjoying every minute of this.

Watching my family celebrate in the street, I can't help but shake my head. Fate certainly has a funny way of working out your life scenes for you. And this scene is one that I'll always remember.

"Let's go eat!" Jax yells out, putting his arm around my shoulders.

Kurt opens the door for us and Wren leads the way, holding a beaming Franny's hand.

After Kurt tells the busboy to get the broom and bucket in order to clean-up the broken glass in front of the car, he pushes through the saloon doors that lead into the kitchen to get our grub.

I sit in my stool, and before I can grab my beer, Francine's arms wrap around me from behind.

"How am I ever going to repay you for all of this, Butch Casady?" She whispers into my ear, causing goosebumps all over my body and a hard dick.

I take a quick sip of Coors, and turn my head so that our foreheads are touching. "I thought we already discussed my preferred currency."

She laughs, licks my ear, and takes her place next to me.

"Keep that shit up, and I promise you won't be eatin' wings..." I warn, stopping the incoming giggle with a kiss.

I can feel Kurt behind me when he says, "Butch, I need you back here." That's a tone I recognize. Shit. There's trouble.

Wren and Jax are already standing from their seats, looking at Kurt.

"I'll be right back, sweetheart," I tell Francine.

She says okay, but she's no fool. I know she's already picked up on the unease. "You boys better hurry up, though. I'm hungry." She grins at us, attempting to lighten the mood.

"You got it, Fran" Jax answers, squeezing her shoulder before we disappear into the kitchen.

Following Kurt to the back, past the oven and steel shelving, we walk into the shared storage and office space. He tells us over his shoulder, "She tried to sneak in through the back door and up to her apartment. But I saw her first."

When he steps aside, I see her sitting there in the old office chair. "Shit."

Kurt's bartender, Gemma, is crouched over in the wheeled office chair, her shirt ripped into pieces, and her face beat to hell. Her tears are mixing with the blood from the slits on her lip, running off her chin and into her lap. The jeans she's wearing are torn and stained with blood.

Jax pushes through and looks at her busted up face and then back to Kurt. "Mick?"

Kurt shakes his head yes, his face murderous, as I kneel and push a lock of Gemma's straight bleached blonde hair behind her ear.

"What happened, sweetheart?"

Refusing to look at us, she keeps her head tucked down, the steady stream of red dripping off her face.

It's been weeks since I've seen Gemma. And a few months since we last slept together. I always knew Gemma wanted more. And I knew I could never give it to her. I had told her as much. So, when Francine entered my life, Gemma quietly left it.

Making a scene isn't her MO, and I had never asked her to, but she stayed clear of KJ's on Wednesday nights. I figured it was for the best.

Kurt had told me she'd been seeing Mick. Everyone in town knows Mick Jackson's a drunk with a nasty temper and a reputation for pushing women around. And considering that's the whole reason Gemma came to work for Kurt in the first place, tryin' to escape the bastard beating her up in Pennsylvania, the fact she was putting herself in that same sort of relationship again makes me feel partially, if not wholly, responsible.

"Gemma, what happened?" I ask, a little more forcefully this time.

Her chin quivers, and she raises her head. The heated fury coming off of all of us at seeing her face in full makes the air in the room thick. "Jesus," Jax says under his breath.

"It's my fault." Not able to open her mouth all the way because of the cuts and bruises, her words are slurred. "I slipped."

"Bullshit," Kurt seethed. "Don't lie for that son of a bitch, Gem. It's not the first time he's done it. And if you don't help us stop him, it won't be the last," he tells her as he walks out of the office, slamming the door open so hard it bounces off the wall and shuts again.

I squeeze her knee a bit, and she looks at me. "You can't just roll over for this shit."

"Please," she pleads. "It was my own fault. I just want to go upstairs to bed."

Kurt comes back into the room carrying a big pouch of ice chips. "Here doll," He says, handing her the bag. "Hold this over your eyes."

"Thanks," she whispers, pushing herself off the chair cautiously. Groaning as she tries to straighten.

"Woah -" I tell her, stopping her from going any further. I pick her up gently in my arms, cradling her back and her arms, "I got you."

"I say we pay Mitch a visit," Wren says as I carry Gemma into the hallway.

"Can't do shit about it if she won't name him," Jax mutters.

"She ain't gonna name him," Kurt says angrily.

"They never fucking do." Jax answers.

"Butch?" Turning around, I find myself looking right at Francine; she is looking right at Gemma.

"What's going on?" Her eyes are shrewd and her voice is deceptively low.

"Franny, I gotta handle this. I need you to wait for me at the bar, yeah?" My question not really a question but more of a statement as I turn on my heel to continue taking Gemma up to her room. Not wanting to get her involved in this crap.

"Um, no," she says, following me up the steps.

"Butch, put me down. I can walk," Gemma argues, clearly trying to avoid adding any more conflict to the situation.

"I'm not puttin' you down until you're in your bed," I tell her. Listening to every step Francine takes behind me.

"It's not locked," mumbles Gemma as we approach her door at the top of the steps. Bending my knees to grab the knob with my hand, I brush against Francine's body next to mine. She opens the door and steps back, allowing me room to get through.

The two apartments above the bar are outdated but clean and both have the same layout. The door opens into the main room. The kitchen is directly ahead to the left, the bathroom in the middle, and the small bedroom to the right.

I walk swiftly past the couch and make a right, pushing the

bedroom door open all the way with my foot.

Carefully, I set her on the bed.

"I'm so embarrassed," she whispers, a whole new stream of tears wetting her face.

"All you gotta do is say it was Mitch," I tell her.

Shaking her head, she starts hyperventilating. "I - I ca - can't."

"Damn it, Gemma! Don't protect him!" I thunder.

Rushing into the room with a stack of towels, a glass of water, and a bottle of pills, Francine looks at me angrily and scolds, "All right, Butch. That's enough." Setting the glass next to Gemma on the bedside table, she drops the towels and medicine down on the bed and turns around with her hands on her hips, her eyebrow cocked, "Why don't you wait for me at the bar, *yeah*?" She says, using my own words back at me.

Getting the idea I'm not going to move, she storms up to me and pushes me out of the room, closing the bedroom door in my face.

"Go downstairs, Butch." She calls to me through the wood paneling.

Sixteen
Got It

I walk down the steps scratching my head.

The boys are still standing together right outside the office. They stop talking when they see me.

Wren, rubbing his neck, says, "Sorry, Butch. There was no stopping that woman." Obviously referring to a hell-bent-on-following-me Franny.

"Where is Fran?" Jax asks, looking around me and up the steps.

"She kicked me out of the apartment. Told me to wait for her down here," I answer honestly. The confusion I feel laced through my voice.

The four of us stand there in that small doorway awkwardly for entirely too fucking long, our hands in our pockets, none of us knowing what in the Hell to actually do, before Kurt finally suggests we wait at the bar. We all agree, I mean, we might as well have a cold beer while we wait.

Nearly an hour passes before Francine finally walks through the swinging doors of the kitchen.

All four of us immediately stand up and wait for her to approach.

"Can I get a white wine, please Kurt?" She asks, sitting in

her stool and crossing her legs.

Kurt rushes around the bar and grabs the bottle from the minifridge, refilling her wine glass. It's quiet as hell in our little group.

Jax and Wren look at me in question. I shrug. I don't have the slightest fucking clue what's happening.

She takes a sip of wine and we slowly surround her. Me on her left, Wren and Jax on her right, and Kurt right across the bar.

"She's sleeping," Franny says, staring down into her drink. Her pink fingernails tap against the side of the glass. "It was Mitch Jackson. She walked in on him and Tina at his house snorting some pretty heavy stuff, among *other* things they were doing. She was upset, he was sky high, and he lost it. Probably worried she'd turn on him and turn him in, he threatened her within an inch of her life; and when he was done proving his point with his fists and feet, he threw her out. She's agreed to file a police report tomorrow morning before she hops a bus to go back home to her parents in PA. What she needs tonight is rest. She has at least three broken ribs, two broken fingers, and her eyes will be swollen and completely shut by morning. Her nose, somehow, is not broken. Just badly bruised. The cuts on her lips will make eating, drinking, talking, breathing, literally *anything,* hell for her over the next week or so."

We stand there with our mouths open in shock. Since when is my woman a fucking nurse? Or Columbo for that matter?

Taking one more sip of wine, like we're not standing around her flabbergasted out of our damn minds, she spins in her stool and unfolds her legs to stand up. The way she handles her body as graceful as always.

"I'm going home," she says, starting towards the door.

"Yeah, okay. Let's go -"

She spins around and puts her hand on my chest, stopping me from finishing my sentence or following her. "No, Butch. *I'm* going home. *You* can stay here and think about how *very* unwise it was to try to keep this from me. If I don't get to shut you out, then you don't get to shut me out. That's how this works." Her hands wave between us, "Otherwise, we don't work."

"Franny -"

"Nope. You don't get to talk your way out of this one. You think I don't know you were sleeping with her?"

Wren coughs, the boys all of a sudden looking at super fucking important things on the ceiling, on the wall, down at their feet, any-fucking-where but me and Francine.

"Is that what you think of me? That I'm some goody-two-shoes that would turn my nose in the air on someone in need just because you were screwing her? That I wouldn't understand why you'd want to help that person? Someone who is standing where," she points to herself to emphasize her point, "*I* was just a few months ago?"

I rock back on my feet. Like a blow straight to my stomach, I realize that the reason she knows so much shit about Gemma's injuries is because she's been in that same damn situation. Self-diagnosing, self-medicating, self-healing at the hands of motherfucker, Stephen.

"You don't get to decide what I do and don't get to know. What I can and can't handle. It's all of it, or it's nothing.

Think on that, Butch." She pushes past me and through the door, leaving me staring at the place she had been.

Kurt breaks the silence when he barks out a laugh. "Well, shit. Butch finally met his match!"

"No shit," I mutter running my hands through my hair.

"Well, I know who to turn to when a victim is withholding information," Jax says, shaking his head in disbelief.

"I knew she was special, but who knew she could be such a firecracker?" Kurt chuckles, cleaning up Francine's wine glass as I sit down.

"What the hell are you doing?" Wren asks me.

I look at him in question.

"What - the hell - are - you - doing?" He asks again slowly as if I can't keep up with what he's saying.

"Well, I can't exactly go home right now," I say, taking a swig of Coors.

"The fuck you can't," Wren says. "You are a fool if you don't follow that woman home and work this shit out."

"Jesus, Wren, you heard her. She doesn't want anything to do with me right now. I mean, what the hell was I supposed to do? And what the hell am I supposed to do now? Beg?"

"On your hands and knees if you have to," Jax says before taking a drink of his beer.

"That woman is nothing but pure class. And if you think you'll ever get a shot like that again, you're a dumbass," Kurt adds.

"You either go fix this, or I'll do it. But I'll be the one she's sleeping next to," Wren threatens.

"I'm the one that found her alongside the road! Had it not been for that damn storm calling me all over the county, I'd have been the one to take her home," Jax says. "Hell, that should give me first dibs."

Throwing down his towel onto the counter, Kurt says, "Well, I've been sitting on a nice little nest egg for some time now. I'm thinking it's plenty enough to keep a woman like that happy. Maybe I'll head on over."

"All right. That's it. Stop talking about how you're going to get my woman in your beds before I kick all your asses." Fuming, I storm out of the bar.

The sound of the guys cheering me on like some kind of moral-fucking-support system has me giving them the finger over my shoulder right before I walk out.

I haven't been this nervous driving home since I stayed out too late drinking with the boys in high school and knew Granny was going to ream my ass.

I pull the truck behind Franny's new car. Her *Lucky Charm*. Jesus, even when she names a damned car, she does it with style.

Dropping my forehead on the steering wheel, I try to think of what I'm going to say to her. And after ten minutes of my brain coming up with exactly no-fucking-thing, I pull the keys from the ignition and hop out.

When I'm on the stoop, my hand on the knob, I hesitate. "Scaredy cat," I whisper to myself.

Quietly closing the door behind me, I kick off my boots, and drape my jacket over the back of the chair. When I look up, I'm startled to find Francine standing in the dining room, barefoot in a pink silk robe that barely covers her ass. Her hair is piled on top of her head and she's leaning against the door jam, her arms crossed, and her expression unreadable.

I wait for her to say something. But she just stares me down, not moving, quiet as a mouse.

Pocketing my hands, I stumble through my first sentence. "I - ah - I know you said for me not to come home, but I - uh - thought maybe we should," I clear my throat, "talk. Maybe we should talk."

Still nothing.

"Gemma, she's one of Kurt's girls. She wound up at KJ's because she was getting tossed around and needed a safe place. A clean slate. I guess I felt, I *feel*, responsible for what she went through tonight. I just didn't feel the way for her she wanted me to when we were ..."

Fucking silence.

"I - well, when I saw her face, I saw red. I still care about her. Like a friend. And I, I mean, I wasn't trying to hide it from you, I just wanted to make sure, I needed to make sure, she was okay."

Abso-fucking-nothing.

"The guys, we protect KJ's girls. I never should have started anything with her. And if I hadn't, she probably would have already moved on to start a better life. So, this is on me."

Nothing.

"Jesus Fran. I really, I screwed up. I - I'm sorry!"

Pushing from the wall, she slinks up to me, sliding her hands up my chest, and back down sliding around my back, untucking my t-shirt. She whispers against my mouth, "Your apology is accepted." She pulls my shirt up and over my head before we're in a full-on lip lock.

She's unbuttoning my jeans and pushing them down my

legs, my cock springing free right in her face.

Placing a kiss on the tip of my dick, she stands up and watches me step out of my pant legs. For every step I take towards her, she takes one back until we're nearly in the dining room.

"This doesn't seem fair. Me naked and you dressed."

"Life's not fair Butchy," she breathes out, her chest rising and falling heavily

I growl, grabbing the sash of her robe and untying it in the process. The robe falls open, revealing a completely naked Francine beneath.

Shrugging her shoulders, she lets the soft fabric swish off her smooth skin, puddling onto the floor behind her.

I lose all control and pull her to me at the same time I've pushed her against the wall. My body rocking against hers, my cock pressed between our bodies. "I don't think I can do anything but fast right now."

Turning her head from my kiss, she inhales air and holds onto my shoulders as my lips and tongue enjoy every inch of her throat. "I like fast," her voice a breathy whisper, "and hard."

She pushes up on her feet, wrapping her legs around my waist, and our mouths find each other again, assaulting and bruising the sensitive skin of our lips with teeth.

Holding her ass cheek in my palm, I grab my cock and lead it right where it loves to be. And once I've pressed in enough, both hands grip her ass. Rearing up and forward, I seat my dick entirely inside of her with a groan.

"God!" Francine exclaims, throwing her head back and wrapping the top of her body against me tightly. Her nails scratch the shit out of my back.

Pressing us both against the wall, she licks, kisses, and bites my neck while I fuck her wet pussy standing. I can hear the picture frames shaking on the other side of the wall in time with each thump and pound.

Francine's holding me so tight that I place my hands on either side of her head and use the friction of my body pinning her between me and the wall to drive into her harder.

She breaks from my mouth to gasp and I feel her pussy contracting against my dick. My movements turn into an erratic hammering of my body against hers; plastered against the wall.

We both come together fast in loud, bellowing convulsions, the spasms of our limbs out of our control.

Resting my head between her breasts, I struggle to come back down from the high. "So, you're tellin' me that all I need to do, in order to get *that*, is apologize?"

Her giggle has my cock still inside her twitching and I groan.

I lift my head and kiss her long and slow and when we come up for air, all laughter from her face gone when she says, "Don't keep things from me, Butch."

"Got it," I tell her as I slowly drop her down to her feet. "Let's get cleaned up and go to bed, darlin'."

Seventeen
Yep

"Franny! We're gonna be late!"

Lou Lou and I have been sitting in the living room for over an hour waiting for Francine to finish getting ready.

"I'm coming, I'm coming. Hold your horses!" She says, her heels clicking on the steps as she comes downstairs.

I look at the clock on the wall. It's ten til seven.

Lou Lou sees Franny round the corner and claps, "Mama!"

Standing up off the couch, I whistle. "You definitely deserve a round of applause, sweetheart."

Turning on her black high heeled toes, Franny spins around with her arms out to give me a view of the entire package.

"God damn," I mutter. The little black dress she's wearing is tight enough to leave me wondering if she even has room for underwear. I pocket my hands to keep from finding out.

"Is it too much?" She asks, picking up Lucy Lou and planting a huge kiss on her cheek.

"Darlin', you could show up to the party in sweatpants and still be the most beautiful woman in the room." I tell her, grabbing her coat draped over the side of the couch.

"We've got to hurry. Party starts at seven." Out of habit, I look down at my empty wrist to check the time.

Setting Lou Lou on her feet, she slips her arm into the sleeve of the coat I'm holding. "It's too bad you still haven't found your watch," Francine says.

"Yep," I answer.

I told her I lost it a few weeks ago, not knowing she was going to tear the damn house apart to try and help me find it. I came home from work one night to a sweaty Francine and a disaster of a house. She'd pulled every piece of furniture out, turned over every pillow, emptied out every cabinet in her attempt to find it. And when she didn't, she stood in the kitchen with tears in her eyes, apologizing. Jesus. The guilt I felt in that moment made my chest hurt so bad, I had a hard time breathing.

"Oh! Don't forget Wren's gift," she reminds me for the twentieth time.

"Put it in the car when I started it up a half an hour ago."

She bends down to zip-up Lucy's coat, and I hand her the little matching pink hat.

Once she's bundled up like a pink marshmallow puff, I pick her up in my arms. "You need to concentrate on walking in those shoes," I say to Franny, my hand on her back.

I buckle Lucy into her car seat and slide into the front seat of the Eagle.

We pull out of our driveway and pull right into Gran's. Wren's parents were okay, but they spent a lot of time fighting. So, he spent a lot of time at our place growing up. Rare was the night that Wren wasn't sitting at Gran's dining room table at dinner.

I honk the horn, "I'm gonna go help her."

As soon as I get to the side door, Granny's stepping out. A wrapped box with a bow on top in her hands. "I got it." I tell her, grabbing the box from her and taking her arm.

Helping her down the driveway and opening the door so she can slide in next to Lucy, I hear her tiny voice squeal in delight, "Danny!"

"Hello, my sweetheart," Granny coo's back as she buckles herself up and I close the door.

"All set?" I ask everyone before I pull out. I've learned my lesson with three women to ask before we leave to go literally fucking *anywhere* because more times than not, someone always forgets something.

Laughing, Francine says, "I think we're good."

"If I forgot something, you can just come back for it," Granny says, tickling Lucy Lou in the backseat.

"Yep." I sigh. It's not worth the fight. And I'd never win it anyway.

Walking into the dark bar, the lights flash on right before everyone jumps out from behind tables to yell, "Surprise!"

When they see it's us, there's a universal moan of disappointment.

"Come on, man!" Kurt yells.

"Not my fault!" I exclaim, following Gran and Francine as they laugh and walk in, saying "Hi" to everyone we pass. "You try to get three women out the door."

All of us take a spot next to Jax against the wall and I pick up Lucy Lou to keep her with us. If she's not in your arms, she'll run all over.

Not one minute later, Wren walks in and everyone

screams, "Surprise." Again. This time to the right person.

The rest of the party- and night- goes off without a hitch, and Lou Lou steals everyone's heart. Especially Wren's. He may talk a big tough-guy game, but he's a sucker for kids.

I'm sitting at the bar watching Lucy Lou pull Wren all around the joint, her whole hand holding one of his fingers, when Granny Jean approaches me from behind, her hand on my back. "I like *this* Butch."

She sits down next to me. "Yeah? And which Butch is that?" I ask.

"The one that has a woman and little girl in his house. The one that doesn't work so late anymore. The one that hasn't stopped watching either of them all night," she answers.

"Hm." I pop a few pretzels into my mouth.

"What happened to your watch?" She nods towards my bare wrist.

I look at my wrist and for a split second, I debate just telling her the truth. "Lost it," I answer, like a coward.

There's a lot to be said about Granny. She may be push-over when it comes to little girls with curly hair clad in all pink, but she's no fool. And she proves it when she quietly says, "She's worth it."

The two of us share a moment of understanding, and I lean over to kiss her cheek.

Granny smiles big. "Butch, I've got to tell you something."

"Oh yeah? What's that?" I ask, throwing a few more pretzels in my pie hole.

"I've been seeing Bobby for a while now and I think he's going to move in with me."

I don't say anything. What the hell am I supposed to say to that?

She squeezes my arm, "Now, I know you probably think it's a mistake. But, I'm tired of being alone." She cackles, "And I'm tired of fighting him off!"

I turn my neck and find Bobby across the room behind us. His bald head glistens and he's smiling through his thick gray mustache. He must feel our eyes on him, because he looks at us. I turn my head back to Gran. "He's not good enough."

Granny laughs and squeezes my arm once more before waving at him. "Bah! Poppycock! He's a good man with his own money. He doesn't need me for anything other than what I need him for."

I don't answer.

"I'm not asking your permission Butch Casady. I'm simply giving you the courtesy of forewarning. And I expect you to be nice to him. After all, he's kept the Quick Mart open late all these years just for you!" I feel like a kid getting lectured. "And, he's good to me." She ends the conversation with that and leaves my side, going in Bobby's direction.

I watch in judgment as he puts his arm around her and am about to go over there and figure out what exactly his intentions are with Gran when someone yells, "Time for presents!"

Everyone starts to meander over to a small high-top table covered in wrapped boxes. Jax pushes Wren through the crowd of onlookers and shoves him into a stool.

Wren's face is red from the attention, but he's a good sport. He's most-likely three sheets to the wind by now.

Lucy Lou picks up the box we brought off the floor and

stumbles over to Wren with a huge smile on her face, the box bigger than she is.

I never did ask Francine what was in the giftbox. I guess that's one of the perks of having a good woman.

Putting down the small present he was going to open, he reaches down and picks Lou Lou up with the box still in her hands, and places her on his lap.

She helps Wren unwrap the blue paper and he smashes the red bow from the top onto the curly mop of hair. Lucy squeals with delight, clapping her hands like it's her own birthday.

And when Wren pulls out a sleek and shiny black and gold Harley Davidson motorcycle helmet, my eyes find Francine standing in the crowd.

She's got her hands clasped in front of her mouth, giddy with as much excitement as Lou Lou while she watches Wren turn the helmet around in his hands. Appreciating the meaning behind the gift.

Yep. We all know he's getting a bike.

And yep. I've got a good woman.

"Thanks, man!" Wren says over the noise of everyone talking. He finds Francine, which is easy to do since she stands out in any crowd, and says, "But I know this was all you, so thanks Fancy Fran!"

Everyone starts busting out laughing at the truth of the joke and Jax punches my arm. "Yeah, we all could have guessed that there's no way you would have thought to buy *and* wrap that!"

I grab my beer and knock his chest with my hand. "Don't be jealous that you don't have your own personal shopper,"

I tease the jerk over my shoulder as I go to Francine.

She's watching Wren open his other gifts, Lou Lou still "helping," and I put my arm around her shoulders.

Thanks to those sexy heels on her feet, her head is closer to mine than normal. She looks up at me and smiles. "Fancy Fran and The Sundance Kid."

"Hm," I mumble, looking at her mouth as my hand roams down her back to squeeze her ass. Those plump pink lips are like a magnet to me, and I lower my head to taste her cherry lipstick.

"You need to fix your lipstick, Fancy Fran," I tell her as I lick my lips clean and squeeze her rear one last time for luck.

EIGHTEEN
THIRTY THOUSAND

"I love my car," Francine sighs, her feet on my lap.

Lou Lou's on the floor playing with her blocks and Francine and I are relaxing on the couch after a long Friday. Dinner's cleaned up, I walked Gran home, Fran gave Lucy Lou a bath, and now we have nothing planned the rest of the night except doing this.

We had just turned on MacGyver when she, once more, confessed her undying love for the set of wheels she drove all over town today.

Chuckling, I warn, "You keep telling me how much you love that car, and I'm going to wind up jealous of a damn station wagon."

She wiggles her toes in my hand and laughs.

Distracted by our banter, Lucy Lou stumbles over to us, her damp curls bouncing with every step and her footed pajamas covered in blue and pink bunnies. She slaps her little hand on my knee, "Dada pick Lou Lou up."

I can feel Francine's legs stiffen across my lap before she pulls them off quickly, sitting up straight. "Oh, no Lou Lou honey -"

Cutting her off, I lift Lucy Lou into my arms, "It's all

right." Setting her onto my lap, and pulling Francine's legs back on it too.

I squeeze her narrow feet and give her a smile, looking back at the tv. Trying my damndest to make it all seem like no big deal, when really, my heart is fucking thundering right out of my chest.

Can anything puff up a man's ego more than the first time they're called dad? I honestly don't think so.

The rest of the night is spent watching Rich Dean Anderson *MacGyver* some shit up, and me watching Lou Lou sleep in my arms and Francine snooze half across my body.

I finally broke down, woke up Franny, and carried Lucy Lou to bed while Francine did all her pre-bed lady crap in the bathroom.

I don't even know what she does in there exactly, but I have a feeling she uses every one of the gazillion bottles of shit she's got in the basket on the counter. And she walks out smelling good with rosy cheeks, a clean face, brushed teeth, and a smile, so I guess it doesn't matter anyway.

We both collapse onto the bed, her butt pushed up against me and my arm slung across her. Not waking up until we hear the sound of a babbling Lucy Lou in the other room the next morning.

"We slept in. Are you hungry?" She whispers, not wanting Lou Lou to know we're awake yet.

I rub my nose into the back of her hair. "Yep. But not for food."

Quietly laughing, she pushes her ass against my hard cock. "Hmm. What are you hungry for, then?"

My hand roves over her body until it's at her crotch. Rubbing my fingers over her panties, I can feel the moisture coating the satin.

Wedging my arm under her neck, I use it to pull her face back to mine so I can lick and suck her ear while I finger her.

She's breathing heavily and pressing hard against me when I hear the phone ring downstairs.

Both of us ignoring it, she grabs my wrist, "Yes, right there," she puffs. Her pink nails dig into my skin.

Reaching behind her with her free hand, she grabs a handful of my hair as she finds her release. Her body pulsates against my hand and I don't stop rubbing even after she's finished. "Butch," she pants, "I can't do it again."

Biting the lobe of her ear, I whisper, "You can."

She's squirming and mewling in my arms and I'm pretty sure I'll have scars from her nails on my wrist. Fuck, this is hot.

Her grip on my head has gone from grounding to punishing, pulling my hair at the root.

Releasing my hair, her hand dives into my boxers, grabbing my cock and stroking hard. She squeezes and pumps my dick, her grasp almost punishing.

My ejaculation comes fast, coating my shorts and her hand. And when she finds her second release, my fingers soaked from her panties, she doesn't do it quietly. She screams my name with her body bucking from the bed.

Pulling my fingers from under the sheets, my arm releases its hold on her neck. Francine lets go of my dick and slides her hand out from my boxer shorts, the cold, wet fabric sticking to my skin.

The phone's ringing again, Lucy Lou's calling out

"Mama!", and we're both out of fucking breath.

"I think she knows we're awake," Francine says.

Bending my arm behind my head, I sit back against the headboard and take a deep, relaxing gulp of air. "Darlin', if we had the windows open, the whole fucking neighborhood would have known we were awake."

Laughing, she gets out of bed and grabs her robe laid across the bottom of the mattress. When she passes by my side on her way to get Lou Lou, she gives me a quick kiss and I grab her breast for a quick squeeze.

I listen to them chatting and hear the sound of Francine's small feet on the steps, going down to start coffee and give Lou Lou a tray full of cereal.

Once I've changed my shorts and taken a piss, I head downstairs to see what the girls are up to.

I'm surprised to find Francine still holding Lucy Lou, no coffee started. She's just standing still at the phone, staring at it.

"Franny?"

"They found me," she says. Her voice sounds incredulous.

Stepping forward quickly, I put my hands on her shoulder so she's facing me, "What are you talking about? Who found you?"

"My parents," she answers simply, reaching out a steady finger and pressing the "Play" button on the answering machine.

The voice over the phone sounds like an eerie copy of my woman's. Just older. And much more pretentious. The clinking and clanking of dishes happening in the background make it obvious that she's using a payphone.

"Francine. This is your mother.

Your father and I have taken time out of our Saturday to drive here to Eddington.

We are at the Bacon and Eggs Diner *and would appreciate it if you could take time from whatever it is you do, to meet us here.*

We will stay until 11. No later. We have engagements at home that we cannot simply skip. You understand the importance of our commitments."

And that was it. That was all the woman, who hasn't seen her daughter in over two years, who has never met her granddaughter, says over the machine.

Shaking her head, Francine's confused, "I don't. I don't understand. How did she find me?"

Pulling the two of them into my arms, I rest my chin on her head. "Eddington's not real big, sweetheart. If they're at *Bacon and Eggs*, I'm sure it just took askin' around to get a location and number for us."

I look at my watch, it's almost ten. Rubbing her arms, I pull back. "So? Are we goin'?"

The diner's only open in the mornings, considering the menu is strictly breakfast food. They close by ten during the work week, but stay open until noon Saturday and Sunday.

"I suppose we should." she answers, not at all looking confident in her decision.

Lifting Lucy Lou from her arms, I place her in the booster. "Why don't you go up and get ready? I'll feed her and get the coffee going."

As if she's in a daze, she just walks out of the kitchen and up the steps. Jesus. I knew her parents were snooty, but I'd have never guessed they had this kind of effect on her.

Once the three of us are dressed and ready, we take Lucy Lou to gran's house and hop in the truck.

The drive to the diner is quiet. Franny gave off some serious, "I don't want to talk" vibes and I am respecting that. I imagine she's trying to get herself in the right headspace for dealing with her parents.

I pull the black beauty into a free spot and pocket the keys.

Franny doesn't move or make any attempt to open her door. "You don't have to do this. We can go right back home if that's what you want."

Finally, she turns her head and looks at me. A sweet smile is on her lips. "No. I can do this. I just need to know what they came here for."

Unbuckling herself, she leans across the bench and grabs my cheek, giving me a kiss. "I'm ready."

I close my door and walk around to hers. I take her hand in mine, put my black wayfarers on my head, and we walk into the busy diner.

She doesn't need to tell me which ones are her parents. They are sitting stoically in a no-doubt sticky booth. Their noses couldn't go up any higher into the air unless they wanted to look straight into the sun.

I recognize pretty much everyone in the joint and nod my head at a few as we pass by.

Approaching the table, Francine squeezes my hand and I return the gesture back. Her mother has spotted us and she whispers into the ear of the business man sitting next to her.

Within seconds, both sets of eyes are on us. Rather, both sets of eyes are on me.

And when we are standing at the table hand in hand, Francine's mother gives her daughter a long, scrutinizing once over. Her eyebrows raised, she takes in what Franny's wearing. Which just so happens to be one of my old sweatshirts, black leggings and a pair of converse tennis shoes.

"Mom, Dad." Francine says in greeting. Neither one of them bothers to get up from their seats.

"Francine." Her mother chides. Her eyes are still on the ratty sweatshirt.

They look utterly ridiculous in this diner. Dressed to the nines like they're heading to one of those fancy charity events that rich people go to with other rich people to eat expensive food and give money to the poor, they are catching the attention of the entire restaurant.

"This is Butch," Franny continues introductions. "Butch, this is Richard and Whitney Whitmore."

Both of us are still standing awkwardly at the side of the table.

I reach out my hand to her father, "It's nice to meet you, Mr. Whitmore."

Looking at my grease-stained hand, her father glances back up at me, making no move to take my offered gesture. The distaste written all over his immaculately shaved face.

It's clear he's not going to shake my hand, so I pull it back, wiping it on my jeans and tucking it into my pocket. This is going fucking swell.

"Is this what you came here for? So, you could judge and condescend?" She's trying to not cause a further scene in the tiny diner, but her voice is clipped and angry. "I don't need this," she says, grabbing my hand. "Come on Butch, let's go home."

"Francine. Sit down." Richard speaks for the first time. His voice is soft but commanding. It's clear he's used to being in charge.

She falters in her step and looks back to them.

"We came all this way to see you, after all," her mother adds.

Her eyes look up at mine and I shrug, letting her decide what happens here.

Hesitantly, she walks back to the table and slides in the booth seat opposite her parents. I squeeze in next to her. Going by the look on her mother's face. She's just as equally unimpressed with my white t-shirt, old jeans, and leather jacket as she was Francine's sweatshirt.

I run my hand through my hair, waiting for someone to start the conversation.

A waitress named Judy with bright red and wearing a blue apron covered in cartoon pictures of bacon and eggs steps up to our table. "What can I get you folks?"

"I'll take a black coffee please," I answer. "Franny, you want an orange juice?" I say, already knowing she does.

"Yes. Please." She says to the waitress with a small smile on her face while her hand comes to rest on my leg under the table.

"Nothing for us," Whitney states haughtily, dismissing the waitress and not even bothering to acknowledge her. Based on the way they're holding themselves right now, I know there's no way in hell they'd actually risk eating or drinking in a place that they believe to be beneath them.

I cover Franny's hand with mine and we both look at her

parents, waiting for them to decide when they're ready to talk.

"So, you've been here?" Her mother inquires, looking around offended.

"For a few months. Before that, Lucy Lou and I were in Higby," she answers.

"Hm," Richard huffs. "And you never thought that maybe it would be in your mother and my best interest in you simply came home?" He questions.

"You know how people talk Francine," her mother chides again.

The waitress returns with our drinks, gets a feel of the tension at the table, and tells us she'll be back to get our orders. I almost laugh out loud. There's a fat chance of that. I'm not sure any of us have an appetite.

"Our reputation is of utmost importance." Whitney says pointedly as she leans over the table, looking at Francine accusingly. "I am sure your father could find you a suitable match." Her eyes graze over me and back to Francine, "willing to overlook your *transgressions*."

It doesn't escape my attention that other than referring to her as "the child", they haven't said a damned thing in reference to Lucy Lou, nor have they actually expressed any interest in actually talking *with* Francine. They've just been talking *to* her.

"I don't need you to find me a husband, mother. And *Lucy Lou* and I are staying here in Eddington," Franny says, emphasizing Lou Lou's name. Good, so she didn't miss the slight either.

"Francine Catherine Whitmore, it's time to put an end to

this foolishness. Your mother and I have let you play your games, and now it is time for you to grow up and make responsible choices. You are coming home so we can fix the problems you've created."

I sit up further in my seat. Unsure if I really care for the tone he's taken with Franny.

"The problems I've created? Are you speaking of my *daughter*?" Francine's face is growing red.

Whitney chimes in. "Francine, you know what's best for all of us."

"You mean what's best for *you*, mother." Francine is shaking her head, "No. I'm not leaving Eddington. And I'm not leaving Butch," she says. Her fingers squeeze my leg.

"How much?" Richard says. And it takes me a moment to realize he's speaking to me.

"Excuse me?" I ask. My brows lower.

"Father!" Francine scoffs.

Ignoring her, he continues his death stare my way. "How much will it take for you to walk out of this diner and forget all of this?" And by *"all of this"* he means Francine and Lucy Lou.

Crossing my arms in front of me, I lean back into the booth. "You've got to be shitting me."

"Ten thousand," Richard says, his hands folded calmly in front of him.

I shake my head in disbelief.

Disregarding my denial, he says louder, "Fifteen thousand." This guy must be fucking joking.

Francine leans over the table, "Father, stop!"

We are gaining the attention of the crowd once more.

Coolly, he says to me, "Think about what you can do with fifteen thousand dollars, son." There's no mistaking what he means. How often does a guy like me get offered such a windfall?

"This is ridiculous," Francine exclaims. "Come on Butch, let's go."

My eyes on Richard Whitmore, I counter, "Thirty thousand."

The look of triumph is all over his face.

Francine's head whips up. "Butch," She whispers. My name coated in the pain she's feeling.

Not taking his eyes from me, Richard reaches into the inside pocket of his expensive tweed blazer, pulling out a checkbook.

"Well, at least one of you is being reasonable," Whitney says under her breath. Fixing and primping her hair.

I watch the man with the same color of hair as Francine and Lucy Lou lick the tip of his fountain pen, fill out the check, and slide it across the table to me.

I don't move. My arms still crossed before me.

"That's all she's worth to you?" I ask coldly.

Busy victoriously tucking the checkbook back into his pocket, his head raises in surprise. Finally assessing that maybe I'm a bit more of an adversary than he believed.

"What's that?" Richard's eyes squint at me in anger.

"She's worth a hell of a lot more than that piece of paper." Placing my hands on the table, I lean in, "Even if you sold every Goddamn thing you own; your cars, your boats, your houses, your fucking fancy clothes, you would *never* meet her worth. And that's not even including Lucy Lou. You'd put yourself in bankruptcy a hundred times trying."

He laughs. "Oh, you're feeling proprietary over the kid now?" Calmly clasping his hands in front of him, he sneers, "You can sit there acting like you'd never put a price on my daughter, but that's exactly what you did isn't it?"

"What's he talking about?" Francine asks me, her eyes full of tears.

"We're done here. Let's go Franny," I say, standing up from my seat and putting my hand out to her. I have yet to find the right time to share with her what happened with Stephen, but I'm sure as hell not going to give Richard the pleasure of doing it in front of him.

Taking my offered hand, she starts to scooch out of the booth when her father stops her, grabbing the arm she still has on the table.

"Ask him about Stephen, Francine. Ask him about the money and the car. I think you'll find that he's not the guy you believe him to be."

She looks up at me wearily, but still uses my hand to stand from the seat.

"And when you realize where you belong, we will be waiting," Richard tells her.

I put my arm around her waist and push Francine past me so we're heading towards the door. "She belongs here. With me." I tell them both.

A malicious grin on his face, Richard says to me after I turn my back on him, "You should have taken the money, son."

Walking out of the diner, Francine's unusually quiet.

"You all right?" I ask her, the sound of the truck starting

loud in the quiet cab.

She's staring out the window. I'm not sure she's going to answer me.

Putting the truck in gear, I barely hear her ask, "What did my Father mean about Stephen and the car?"

Shit. Here we go. "Franny, you've gotta understand..."

I'm cut off by Joe's voice on the CB radio. "Sundance. You there? Been trying to reach you for an hour, man. We've got a pretty bad crash over in Parksville. It's gonna take all our trucks."

I pick up the mic, "I'm here. Over."

Joe immediately responds, "We're going to need you, man. This one's bad. Over."

"I just need the location," I tell him speeding up. I still need to drop off Francine, get to the garage to pick up my tower and drive the forty minutes to Parksville.

There's a moment of static before he answers, "Smith Road between Boulder and Junket."

"10-4. Over and out," I finish, turning onto my road and attaching the mic to the cradle.

I stop halfway up the driveway and leave the truck running, "We'll talk later. Yeah?"

Opening her door, she almost shuts it without saying anything to me. But at the last minute, those blue eyes look up to mine and I feel an overwhelming sense of unease. Maybe I should turn the truck off and stay here to work this shit out.

"Okay, Butch," she mutters and shuts the door, walking around the corner of the house.

Dammit.

The sound of the guys giving their ETA's over the radio

puts my ass back in gear. I reverse the truck and floor it down the road.

Nineteen
Are They Here?

I have to fight to keep my eyes open the whole way home.

Once I finally showed up to the wreck site this afternoon, I walked into a complete disaster. Multiple casualties, a shit-ton of injuries, and ten vehicles for my guys to tow all over the tri-state area.

An entire cluster fuck pile-up on the highway caused by an older gentleman that shouldn't have been driving in the first place and will now never drive again.

Pulling the truck behind Francine's car, I can see in the headlights that the green Eagle is still in the same spot it was when I left.

The breakfast with her parents must have stressed her out even more than I thought since she clearly didn't take Lucy Lou to their regular Saturday afternoon story time.

Walking in, the house is quiet and dark. The clock on the stove reads 12:24. It may be a few minutes off, but it's right for the most part.

I quietly close the door, assuming the girls are sound asleep upstairs, and flip the switch on the wall to turn on the light above the table. As I'm slowly kicking off my boots, my stomach growls in protest. Of course, I'm starving. I didn't

173

have time to even stop to piss all day.

Sighing, I rub my eyes and open the fridge. I'm surprised to find no leftovers from whatever dinner was tonight. "Damn," I mutter. There are almost always leftovers. Until I eat them for lunch the next day, at least.

Closing the door, I trudge through the dining room and up the steps. Deciding I'm too damned tired to even make myself a bowl of cereal.

I make a pitstop in the bathroom to handle my business and take a quick shower. If I weren't so filthy and greasy, I'd just fall into bed, but I know Franny won't appreciate the dirty sheets.

I'm showered and practically in the bed before my head catches up with my eyes and I notice the comforter is still pulled up and made from the morning.

Confused, I go to Lucy Lou's room and stand at her door. Her bed is empty, too. I flip the light switch and look around the small room.

There are toys on the floor and the only thing missing from her bed is her favorite blanket. I turn back and flip the light switch in my bedroom.

"Franny?" I call out as I check the spare room. It's dark and empty, just the few boxes on the floor that have been in there since I moved in.

Bounding down the steps, a bad feeling in my gut, I walk through the living room and into the family room, turning on lights along the way. "Francine!" I call out, already knowing that no one is here.

Back in the kitchen, I see the manilla envelope on the counter that I must have missed in my exhaustion when I first came in.

Uptight and uneasy, I unclasp the metal prongs and pull out the stack of papers stuffed inside, causing a small hand-written note from Francine and five black and white pictures to fall out.

My hands slightly trembling, I read the letter with the familiar writing first,

I trusted you.
I am sorry we disrupted your life.
Thank you for everything you've done for us.
Francine

Fuck.

Looking at the pictures, three of the still shots are unmistakably me and Gemma. We're going at it against the wall in the back of KJ's, and in one I've even got her thigh in my hand, pulling her close to me. Another shows me on the back steps lookin' like I'm following her up to the apartments. And the last two are from the day I met Stephen at the truck stop. In one, it appears that I'm taking an envelope from him. The envelope full of cash that *I* gave *him*. In the other, the shithead is driving off in the yellow Pacer and I'm standing outside the restaurant with Jax watching him go. All the pictures are marked with a date and time stamp. And all the dates and times are well after Francine and Lucy Lou rolled back into town and into my life.

There is a stapled stack of papers that are basically a typed-out play-by-play of my schedule from the son of a bitch her parents must have hired to trail me. By the looks of it the PI has been following me around for weeks.

In the other stapled stack is my entire fucking life. My

high school transcripts, my credit, my traffic tickets, parking tickets, bank account information. Jesus, even my criminal record from juvie is in here.

"Fuck!" I yell, throwing the papers across the room. I take a deep breath and run my hands through my hair, trying to figure out what in the hell to do.

Racing through the house and back up the stairs, I start opening Francine's drawers. I open the closet doors. Everything is there. She didn't take anything.

I do the same thing in Lucy Lou's room. All her pink and purple outfits, pajamas and socks are still there.

Slamming the last drawer closed, I pick up the toy block on the floor. My head is spinning. I yell again, throwing the block and punching my hand through the door.

Granny Jean's! Maybe she went next door! I pull my hand out of the wood, my knuckles splintered and bleeding.

Bounding down the steps and into the kitchen, I throw on my boots. Running out and around the house, I pound on Gran's door. "Gran! Gran open up!"

Shit! I should have brought the spare key.

I'm just about to run home to get it when the door opens. Gran's in her blue bathrobe with her hair up in pink foam curlers. "Butch? What's wrong? What happened?" She asks, panicked.

"Are they here?" I ask, pushing my way past her.

She follows me through the small house as I check each room. "Butch! Who? Is who here?"

Falling onto her orange and brown plaid couch from my childhood, I bend forward and hold my head in my bloody hands. "She left," I whisper. "She left me."

"Where's the baby, Butch?" I don't miss the strain in her voice.

Not looking up, I tell her, "Lucy's gone, too."

Granny Jean takes a sharp inhale of breath and grabs her chest, fisting her robe, "Oh no."

Concentrating on breathing, I stand up. "I'm heading home. Sorry for waking you."

"What? Well, what now? Now what are you going to do?" She asks, quickly following behind me to her door.

"I'm going to go home and go to bed Gran. And so should you," I mutter, my hand on the knob.

She's stuttering. "That's it? You're just going to let her go?"

I open the door and step out onto the stoop. "Yep. She made her decision," I say before closing the front door behind me.

In a daze, I walk home. I don't remember when I fell asleep, but it was somewhere between beer ten and eleven.

It feels like I just closed my eyes when the phone in the kitchen rings.

Damn, it's fucking bright in here. My eyes barely open, I fall off the couch and land on the pile of beer cans on the floor. "Shit," I mumble, trying to stand up.

After a few tries, I finally stand myself up straight enough to walk and shuffle into the kitchen, scratching my stomach.

My head is pounding as I pick up the receiver. "Yeah."

There's no one on the other end. "I didn't want to talk to you anyway," I groan. Slamming the phone back on the cradle. It falls off immediately and I have to put it down three more times until it finally latches and stays.

Deciding that I was better off sleeping, I start to trudge back into the family room when the shrill phone rings again.

Now I'm pissed off. "Yeah?" I yell into the phone on the second ring.

"Good, you're awake." Granny's no-nonsense tone says through the line. "Now, what is going on? Where did the girls go and when are you going to get them?"

I hit my head against the wall. And then did it again and again and again. I don't want to think about this. I don't want to talk about this. "Granny, I've got to go. I'll call you later."

I'm halfway to hanging up when I hear her yelling through the phone, "Butch Casady, you better not hang up on me young man! You either talk to me now, or I come over there and you talk to me face to face! *After* I hit you upside the head!"

Slowly, I start to put the phone back to my face but drop it. The handset hits the ground and the coiled cord makes it bounce like a bungee line.

"Shit." Picking the jumping piece of crap phone up, I hold it to my ear. I don't know what to say to Gran. Too hungover to overthink it, I tell her, "I screwed up. She left. I imagine she went home to her parents. And I'm not going after her."

And with that, I hung up the phone, closed the shades all through the house, and found my way back to the couch.

I had already told everyone at the end of the shit day we had yesterday to take today off. And I have big plans to spend the entirety of my free day on the couch - either drinking or sleeping.

TWENTY
THIS AIN'T IT

"Jesus, Joe! Get it fucking together!"

I'm screaming at the guy over the sound of all three diesel trucks running idle in the parking lot. There's been another multiple vehicle accident just outside of Hilford and I had to call Joe in even though it's his day off. Two of my guys are on vacation, so Wren's stepping in to help out and Joe just graced us with his presence - 20 minutes late. Some excuse about the kid being sick and throwing up all night.

"Sorry, Sunny. I didn't sleep at all last night." Joe tells me as he jogs over to his truck.

"Yeah, well, we've all got shit going on. Doesn't mean we can just roll into work whenever we fucking want to." I hop in my truck and slam the door, pissed as hell.

I roll down my window and yell out, "Let's go!" Pulling onto Main Street, the other trucks follow.

The job goes by as uneventfully as possible and we're pulling back into the garage late in the afternoon after dropping off the towed loads to the mechanic in Hilford. Summer's around the corner, and Wren's place is busy as hell with fixing the bodywork and undercarriage of all the cars damaged in the snow, salt, and potholes that come along

179

with winter in the Midwest. He's thrilled as shit that this lot wasn't taken to his shop.

Joe's already in his own car and pulling out of the lot by the time Wren and I are out of our trucks and walking into the garage.

"Jesus. He didn't waste any time," I grumble on my way to the bathroom. One of the worst things about being out on the road all day is the lack of facilities. No big deal if you don't mind stopping at truck stops and gas stations. I'd rather not - unless I'm desperate.

Wren's sitting on the old vinyl truck bench I use for spare seating in the garage.

I pass by him, pull out two beers from the fridge, and circle back to hand him one. It's been a long day and we're both beat from the drive. Cracking them open, we both take a few swigs. I lean against an old table and look down at the grease covering my arm.

"So, when are we going to talk about her?" He asks like the two of us have just been sitting here shooting the shit all damn day.

"We're not," I answer, knowing exactly who "she" is and not taking the bait, swallowing another mouthful of Coors.

He nods with his lips pursed like he's thinking real hard about something. "Makes sense. I mean, after all, you only sleep for shit, drink instead of eat and are an asshole to literally every-fucking-one that has the misfortune of having to be around you - Granny Jean included. And let's not get into what a dumpster fire your house is right now or the fact that you haven't shaved in what...how long has she been gone?" He places his empty beer can down on the floor and looks pointedly at the beard covering the lower half of my face. "Nah. You're right. You're good."

You have got to be kidding me right now. "I don't want to get into this, Wren," I answer in warning. The pissed-off-ness in my tone is clear.

"See, that's the problem with you." He jabs a finger at me, not taking my hint of fuck the hell off.

"Oh yeah? And what's that?" I inquire hotly, putting my own empty can down on the dirty table behind me.

Wren stands up. "You haven't said shit since she left. You also haven't done shit about it. You're fucking miserable, and you're a fucking coward."

I push off the table. "You don't know what the hell you're talking about," I tell him while taking a deliberate step towards him.

"I know you fucked up. I know you know it. And I know that instead of going after her, you're sitting around here like an egotistical cocky son of a bitch that thinks he's pullin' the wool over everyone's eyes." He leans forward towards me. "FYI - you're not."

I push his shoulder. "Why don't you shut the fuck up and worry about your own miserable life. When's the last time you thought about Sandy? Oh, wait. I know. Probably this morning while you were jacking off to her memory." I know that was a low blow. Sandy was Wren's high school sweetheart that up and left town, and him, for some jackass wannabe big shot with a bank full of money and a bright wealthy future. And completely destroyed Wren's heart in the process.

Wren's right hook has always been good. And I can tell

you, based on the fist that meets my jaw, it's still fucking brutal.

When the five Wrens in front of me finally disappear and there's only one left, I see he's ready and waiting for a fight. His fists up and his body in position.

"I'm not fighting you," I mutter, rubbing my jaw and walking away. I need ice.

"The fuck you're not." He answers, hitting me across the back of my head.

I trip up and nearly fall to the ground. "I'm not fighting you," I grit out as I regain my balance and try to walk away again.

"Yeah, that's right. Butch Casady is a fucking pussy ass coward. No wonder she left you. You aren't man enough for a woman like her."

All I see is red. And I don't know how or when it happened, but I've got Wren down on the filthy cement floor, my arm across his neck in a chokehold.

"You don't think I know that?" I seethe into his face. Spit coming out of my mouth with my rage. "That I could never provide for her like she needed? That I wasn't good enough? You don't think I don't fucking miss them every minute of every damn day?"

The tears in my eyes almost fall out. But I press down into Wren's neck one last, hard time before pushing off of him and standing up. Taking a deep breath, I run my fingers through my hair.

"And there it is." Wren says, still laying on the ground. He sits up on his ass and drapes his dirt-covered arms on the top of his bent knees. "Now the real question is, when are you going to realize the first half of all that is bullshit and the last is something you can fix?"

I sigh and put my hands on my hips. Tipping my head back, I close my eyes. I'm so damn tired. "She left, Wren. She chose to believe what she saw on those papers and go back to the life she was raised to live. I'm sure she's engaged to a fancy-ass banker or some shit by now." I look down at him. "I screwed up."

"Yeah, you did." He said, standing up and brushing the dirt off his ass. "But so did her parents. And no one's callin' them out." And with that, he walked out the garage door and left.

My best bud leaves me with a headache and more fucking confused than ever.

Frustrated, I lock up the garage and head home. Pulling the truck in front of the mailbox, I grab the mail for the first time in days and reverse into the driveway.

Bobby's just getting out of his car in Gran's driveway across her front yard as I'm pulling back. I make eye contact with him for a brief second. Just long enough to see him hesitantly wave in my direction before he's out of my view.

He moved in with Granny at the beginning of the month- or maybe it was last month- and to be honest, I don't like it. I barely ever see her anymore and when I do, she wants us to all spend time together like some fucking happy episode of senior citizen Brady Bunch. Thanks, but I'll pass.

To be fair, I have not exactly been much in the mood for anyone's company. I haven't been to KJ's in what seems like forever. And no matter how many times Jax or Kurt call, I don't call back. The only reason I see Wren is because my business is kinda tied to his.

I kick the back door closed with my boot and throw the mail on the kitchen table. Empty beer cans roll off when the pile lands and they scatter loudly onto the floor.

Not bothering to take off my boots, I open the fridge, grab a beer, and chug it. Lifting the pizza box that's been sitting on the stove for a few days, I grab the last slice of meat lovers before I head into the family room to continue my evening routine of sitting my ass on the couch and watching tv while drinking beer until I pass out.

Belching, I kick off my boots onto the carpet, throw my stained shirt onto the floor, and get settled in for the night.

After a few hours of back-to-back Knight Rider episodes, I get up to piss and see the pile of mail on the table that I took from the box earlier and then promptly forgot about.

Sorting through the stack, most of it is junk. And bills. But there's one envelope that catches my eye with its professional typing and official post office seal. It's made out to me and the return address is a business park in Clarks Grove.

Not knowing what to expect when I start opening it, my chest feels tight and my throat is suddenly dry.

I open the folded piece of paper on the top containing three short lines typed on Whitmore House letterhead:

"On behalf of Richard Whitmore,
to cover all expenses accrued by Ms. Francine Whitmore dur-
ing her brief stay in Eddington, Ohio."

Shell shocked, I hold the check in her daddy's name for ten grand.

Putting the check down, I slowly open the second pack of folded papers on the same fancy-assed letterhead.

It takes me a few rereads to realize that what I have in my hands is a Non-Disclosure Agreement and a Protective Order made just for me represented by Richard Whitmore's very own attorneys.

The Non-Disclosure Agreement is to be stamped with my John Hancock and sent back immediately as an acknowledgement of the check received for my "expenses accrued" thanks to her generous father followed by a prompt removal of any memory I have of Francine Whitmore and her daughter Lucy Whitmore.

And the Protective Order is to ensure that I don't go and accidentally forget that I forgot them. Citing my "*personal and professional involvement with a dangerous felon and convicted drug dealer, a Mr. Stephen James Black. Receiving and reselling stolen property* (AKA returning the stolen piece of shit Pacer Francine took *from* Stephen *back* to Stephen Assfuck Black - who apparently had lifted it from someone else. Now all his dumbass confusion at the truck stop that day makes a hell of a lot of sense. He never put the APB out on the car. Whoever the original owner was did.). *Using* Butch's Towing Co. *equipment to apprehend stolen vehicle and knowingly harboring said stolen property at the commercial building of* Rollin' Right, *owned by a Mr. Wren Scout.*" And, as if that wasn't enough, the real shit kicker at the end: "*To protect the safety and well-being of Ms. Francine Whitmore and Ms. Lucy Whitmore.*"

Meaning, if I don't sign this shit, and promise to stay away from Francine, than the mother fucker will not only go after me, but my business and livelihood. And Wren's too. No doubt Dick Whitmore has enough money to take us for all we've got. Best case scenario bein' we rot in a jail cell with a bed and three hot plates a day. Worst case, we're homeless and living under a bridge.

I may not have known what to expect. But I do know - this ain't it.

Kicking cans out of my way as I cross the kitchen, I pick up my phone and punch in the numbers.

It takes a few rings, but he eventually answers. "Jax Finn."

"I need you to get me the home address of Richard Whitmore. And I need to see you."

If he was surprised to hear from me, he didn't show it. Jax said he'd stay in his office for lunch so I could see him sooner rather than later. I don't shower, but I do put on one of the less dirty shirts in the laundry pile.

"Jesus, Butch. You look like shit," is Jax's way of greeting when I walk in the station.

"Yeah, I feel it, too." I answer honestly, following him through the main area and into his office. I put the envelope I brought down on his desk and take a seat in one of the shitty chairs across from it.

He picks it up and immediately notices the return address. "May I?" He asks, brows raised, regarding the envelope.

"Yep."

He lifts the flap and dumps everything out on his desk. The picture that lands at the top of it all is the one of Gemma and I seemingly dry humping each other in the back room of KJ's. He sorts through everything in the pile - the pictures, the investigative report, the check, the Non-Disclosure Agreement, The Protective Order - all of it.

After a long ass time of him reading and me watching him read, Jax finally talks to me. "Seeing as how I haven't seen hide nor hair of you since she left," he pointedly looks at me sarcastically due to the hair on my head and face being drastically overgrown. "I'm going to make some wide assumptions here." He starts flipping through the reports as he's talking to me, "Daddy Whitmore tailed you - dug out whatever he could on you - twisted it to fit his narrative - sent it to Francine - she believed it - left you -" That last one hurt. It's true, but it still hurts like hell. "Surprisingly, his plan worked and now, good ol' Richard realizes he's got some loose ends still untied that could hurt the family business - so he's coming after you - and Wren from the looks of it - and he's trying to bribe you into agreeing." He's holding up the check. "That about sum it up?"

"Yep."

"Hm," looking back down on all the shit all over his desk. Jax picks up the pictures, "Please, for the love of God, tell me that these are not what they seem to be."

"Hell no. Gemma followed me back there that night, I denied her, and she went upstairs alone. I didn't cheat on Francine." The last sentence comes out between my teeth.

"Good." Jax says. His mom slept around on his dad through his entire childhood and they guy doesn't take well to the whole infidelity thing. "And you obviously have no intention of signing these?" He asks in regards to the legal forms.

"Nope."

"Good. Let me look into this guy." He picks up the papers

and shuffles them together in a neat pile, tapping the bottoms on his desk. "In the meantime, do us all a favor and go find yourself a razor, Butch."

TWENTY-ONE
I JUST CAME FOR THIS

The throttle and growl of my old Harley echoes back and forth between the pristine white mansions on Magnolia Street.

It was a beautiful, sunny day when I woke up this morning and I thought, what the hell. If I'm going to go all the way out to Clarks Grove, I might as well take the bike.

Jax called me bright and early yesterday with a helluva lot on Richard Whitmore. After only three days of sniffing around, my buddy came back with a crapload of interesting and not so interesting facts about Dick W. The general shit that I don't care about: 62, been married 40 years, has had many, many side pieces a lot younger than Whitney, Francine is their only child.

And then the shit I needed to know: Turns out, just last year, his banking firm, Whitmore House, was under fire for suspicious accounts and clientele in Switzerland, huge contributions to shady political campaigns, and some confusing tax shit. Point being, he's been a bad boy with money that's not entirely his and Pandora's Box was about to be blown wide open. But, right before the findings made it to national print, Whitmore up and generously donated to the Fraternal

Order of Police, the Association of Newspapers and Publishers, as well as NOVA (an organization for victim assistance). He furthered his righteous and straight-laced image by publicly, and falsely, claiming his own daughter was an unfortunate victim of sexual assault and bravely decided to keep the baby that had been conceived through the horrific events.

So, overcome with all their public feelings and sadness for his beloved daughter, the media, naturally, wanted to see how Francine Whitmore and her baby fared. Dick was running out of excuses as to why she hadn't been seen for some time and he grew desperate. Francine and Lucy Lou needed to be safely stationed inside the homebase, Stephen Black needed to be handled, and so did any dealings Francine had in Eddington.

With Francine back in Clarks Grove and having already handled Stephen - he was arrested for vehicle theft shortly after our little breakfast date - all of his boxes were checked.

Except the one next to my name.

Finding the address Jax had given me, I turn onto the brick horseshoe driveway and ride up until I'm smackdab in front of the huge double doors of the house. Using my foot to kick down the jiffy stand, I remove my helmet and once I'm off the bike, place it on the seat as I look up at the place Francine grew up in.

It may be huge and fancy, but even in the bright sun it seems cold as shit.

I take the three wide brick steps to the landing at the front door in one jump and put my wayfarers on top of my head. Ringing the gold-plated doorbell, I tuck my hands in my jean pockets and step back to take in the immaculately manicured bushes on either side.

I look behind me, making sure to check my surroundings per Jax's order. Something about armed bodyguards on Whitmore duty 24/7.

The tall, thin man that opens the door is in a black penguin suit. A bona fide butler straight out of the movies. Even the way he turns his nose up at me standing here in my leather jacket is fucking cinematic.

"May I help you?" He asks while his long, pointed nose dips down to take in all that's me. His uppity British accent is thick and haughty.

I look behind him into the grand entryway of the house. The sun is hitting the huge crystal chandelier hanging from the ceiling in the center of the room. The marble floor and white, shiny walls glisten in the prism reflections. A huge, imperial staircase sits against the far-left wall with large, ornate frames that hold paintings covering the expanse all the way up to the second floor. My guess is those paintings, each a rendering of some patriarchal guy or gal, are generations upon generations of Whitmore's.

"I'm here to see Francine Whitmore." I say, my eyes having seen their fill of the screaming opulence in front of me.

Not moving, the tightass, entirely too dressed up for a job involving cleaning shit, just stands there and scrutinizes me. I raise my brows, about to repeat my request, thinking maybe he didn't understand my poor-boy English when he starts to close the door. "Wait here," he says right before the door shuts in my face.

It's not too long before he opens the big heavy door once

more and steps aside to allow me in, "Follow me."

So, I follow him. He turns right and walks like he's got a stick up his ass, stopping in front of an intricately carved wood door. Knocking twice, he stands tall and straight, opening the door and once more stepping aside to let me in.

Once I've cleared the doorway, he closes me into the Pine Sol-smelling room.

"Butch Casady. We meet again."

His phony tone implies that we enjoy one another's company.

Richard Whitmore, impeccably dressed with his balding brown hair oily and slicked back, is sitting at a dark wood desk that's almost as wide as the room we're in. There are three phones on the desk and a lot of paper, books, and fountain pens. Everything a guy like him would need to look important while sitting there doing nothing.

Not surprised that he isn't going to allow me to see Francine, I pocket my hands and just stare at him.

"Please." He gestures to one of the overstuffed chairs that face him, "take a seat."

"I'd rather not."

"A drink then. For your trip?" He asks, standing up and tucking his absurd pink tie neatly in his dress coat before gesturing to the bar by the window. His back turned to me, he pours a finger of single malt scotch and lifts it up in question.

"Ah, no, thank you." Reaching into my leather jacket, I pull out the envelope and hand it to him. "I just came for this."

He takes the thick square cut glass of scotch, and my envelope, and returns to his seat. Unbuttoning his dress coat once more and adjusting into his oversized chair in a practiced routine.

"Everything's final then?" He asks, lifting his glass to his lips without lifting his eyes to me. Just a businessman doing business with someone not worth his time.

It figures the conceited asshat assumes that I took the money and signed the forms. It doesn't even occur to him to open the envelope and check the fucking papers.

"Yep," I answer. "All your papers are there." He shakes his head up and down, setting the envelope aside and picking up whatever he was working on before I walked in. Probably about to "dismiss" me.

Tucking my hands back in my pockets, I add, "And so is your check." That gets his attention. "Yeah. See, I didn't want your money then, and I don't want your money now."

His lip curls and his movements are rigid as he opens the envelope and pulls out the folded papers. Flipping through the forms aggressively, he ridicules, "You didn't sign any of these."

"No. I didn't. You may be able to buy and bully your way through life, but I guess I've never been one to roll over and take it up the ass."

He throws the papers down in front of him in disgust. "What is it that you want?"

"I want to see Francine," I shrug my shoulders and answer as though it's obvious.

He snorts. "That's not possible."

I cross my arms in front of me. "Then I'll wait."

"Any business you had with my daughter has long since

concluded. You have been offered two very bounteous amends for your *assistance* and have ignorantly declined both. I am sure you understand that I would not be very successful if I was in the business of offering unmerited handouts to a no one off the street *three* times. Now you're looking at prison, son."

I snort back. "See, that's the problem. I say I want to see your daughter and you automatically assume I have some ulterior motive to get more from her than you're offering me. Not everything is about money, Richard. And I'm not scared of prison."

I step right up to his cherry desk fit for a king. "And let's not ignore the fucking irony of it all, considering when I found Francine and Lucy Lou, they had nothing but the clothes on their backs, escaping a dangerous situation, *scared and on their own*, because *you* turned her out." I cock my head to the side and lean in to his space. "I guess his fallen daughter wasn't deserving of Richard Whitmore's renowned *generosity*. I'm sure the New Yorker and the Wall-street Journal would eat this story up. Speaking of the press, how are your friends in Switzerland?"

Understanding my meaning, the man finally loses what's left of his composure. "You dare speak to me this way in my own home? Get out!" Richard yells. His face growing redder by the second, he stands up from his office chair and slams his hands down on his desk.

Standing straight, I ask, "What's the matter, Dick? Did I say something you don't like? You think you can threaten *me* in *my* home and there won't be any pushback because I'm just some guy off the street?"

I hear the door open behind me, but I don't move from where I'm at. "Where were you when they had no place to go? If you could afford to hire someone to follow me, you sure as hell could have found her a fuckuva lot sooner than you did you pompous bastard! You only came after her because you realized her being gone could be detrimental to your image!"

"GET HIM OUT!" He bellows, shaking and pointing to the door. "You'll regret ever threatening me! I'll take everything you have! Someone call the police!"

The butler tries to pull my arm but I easily break away from his weak grip. "I know my way out," I tell him over my shoulder, a calm smile on my face to mask the fucking rage of fire I feel inside.

There's a hallway full of house staff in black suits and dresses standing around in shock when I leave the private office. I'm sure they're not used to their big boss conducting this sort of business.

Almost to the door, I get a tickling on the back of my neck and the sudden urge to turn around. When I see her standing at the top of the steps, my heart practically pounds straight out of my chest. She's wearing a blue dress and her hand is on the banister as if she was contemplating coming down. Her hair is pulled back into a bun and her face shows no emotion at seeing me standing in her family's mansion hallway. "Franny!" I quickly close the distance towards the bottom of the steps but Richard's henchmen have finally shown up from whatever corners they hide in, roughly yanking me back. They drag me to the door and I struggle against their hold. "I WANT HIM OUT!" Richard yells from his office door.

Fighting for a few extra seconds of time, I plead, "Franny! Listen to me. He's lying! You don't know everything that happened!"

I'm tossed out the door like a bag of trash, and I roughly roll down the brick steps. My leather coat and jeans keep me from sustaining a bad case of road rash, but my pride had no cushion. Quickly, I find my feet and get one last look at my woman before the door closes and she's worlds away. "I love you, Franny!"

Getting on my bike and riding away knowing that Francine and Lucy Lou are right on the other side of those brick walls is one of the hardest fucking things I have ever done in my life.

And knowing that that was probably the last time I'd ever see her, hurts a hell of a lot more than I want to think about.

I don't know if Richard will make true of his threats to me and Wren, and right now, I don't give a fuck.

Not ready to go back to my lonely house, I just drive.

Owning the wind, my bike under me and the sky above me, is probably the best therapy I could get. And by the time I roll back into my drive, racing the summer thunderstorm gathering in the distance, I feel a little lighter. Not better. But less like my heart's been ripped from my chest and I'll never breathe right again.

So, I guess it's progress.

TWENTY-TWO
LUCKY DOG

The first thing I did when I got home from Clarks Grove was walk around my house with a trash bag.

Okay, four trash bags.

I mean, it's not like it's spotless, but I was raised to take better care of my shit. I've never allowed myself to live like that before, and I'll never let myself do it again. I've got more pride than that.

The next thing I did was call Gran with my tail between my legs and apologize for being such a dickhead and ask if she wanted to meet me at Bacon and Eggs the next morning for breakfast. With Bobby.

And the third thing I did was try to move on from what I was thinking my life was going to be. I don't miss Francine and Lucy any less, but with each day that passes, it doesn't sting as much.

I haven't touched Lucy's bedroom or removed Francine's things from mine. I'm not quite there yet. Maybe sometime soon. I'm sure if I packed it up, Kurt would take it and store it in the back of the pub for one of the girls that come through KJ's. Every once in a while, I'll find myself standing in Lucy's room, looking around. And all too often I open

197

a dresser drawer just to get a whiff of the sweet smell of Francine that still covers her shit. But I guess it's not really her shit. I'm sure she's got dressers and closets four times bigger than what she had here filled to the brim with the most expensive threads money can buy.

There's a fourth thing I did, I guess.

And right now, it's licking the shit out of my face while I try to lay down in the driveway and give my Harley a tune up.

"Lucky, come on girl, take it easy." I gently push the Labrador's face away from mine.

I had heard through Bobby that the local pet store was having a dog fair a couple weeks ago. Apparently, all local breeders and rescue agencies come together in the park to show the town what animals they've got that need homes.

Nothing better to do that day, I rode my bike to the park and walked around to look at all the pups and kittens. But when I passed by the cage that held the tiny ball of black, and saw that her name tag posted on the metal bars read "Lucky," well, I couldn't resist kneeling down to get a closer look. And after I got a closer look, and she was licking the finger I had pushed through the opening, I couldn't resist the opportunity to hold her. And once I held her? Well, let's just say that's precisely how they get suckers like me to buy a damn dog.

So, I rode home an hour later with less money in my wallet and a black furball tucked tight into my jacket. Lucky dog.

But it hasn't been all bad. It's actually been kind of nice to have company when I get home from work. She's always happy to see me, loves to play, and sleeps at the end of my bed.

I put down my wrench and tug Lucky over to me, laying on my back and burying my face in her thick, soft coat. She's growing fast but she's still a small fluff of a thing. "You want to play?" I tease, petting her dark black sides.

She's yapping her head off, jumping all over me, and I can't help but laugh.

"You spoil that dog."

I open my eyes to see Granny standing over me and I smile. "That's funny coming from the lady that lets a small cat run her house."

She smiles back and pets Lucky, who's so excited to have company she's whining.

"I just came over to wish you a happy birthday," Gran says, handing me a small wrapped box all while still showering her grand pup with love.

I sit up on my ass and take in her latest sweatshirt creation. All the ladies at card night have been going crazy over these small bottles of paint that they use to decorate their clothes. And Granny Jean's modeling one of them yet again. This one is a bright pink sweatshirt with a big cartoon sunshine shape wearing black sunglasses that covers the whole front of her body. And as always, it's a treat for the eyes. "Ah, Gran. You didn't have to get me anything."

"Poppycock! Of course, I'm going to give you a present on your birthday, you fool!"

I open the box and find a stud collar for Lucky with a nameplate that has my address and phone number.

"In case she decides to run too far," Gran says around Lucky's head because she's letting the dog kiss her face.

I pat my thigh and call for my dog, "Come here girl." She bounds back to me and I wrap the collar around her neck, tightening the strap to fit.

"Thanks. It's great." I say to her, rubbing Lucky's head and ears.

"I wish you'd change your mind about dinner," she says, hitting me with those sad eyes she gets every once in a while when she looks at me.

"I'm going to KJ's. I'll be fine. You know I don't like to make a big deal. Plus, you and Bobby meet up with your church friends on Tuesday nights."

She rubs my head the same way she was just rubbing the dog. "I know, you stubborn mule. But I'd be willing to skip it for you." She bends down and kisses my cheek. "Have fun, Butch. Go take a shower."

I chuckle. "Yes ma'am. Lucy, stay," I command, knowing she'll try to follow Gran back across the yard to her house. I swear the dog has dreams about finally catching that damn cat that taunts her through the windows.

I clean up my tools that are scattered over the cement driveway and put them away in the garage before I head inside with my dog to take a shower.

Cleaned up with a fresh set of clothes, I run my hands through my wet hair. "You need to eat, girl?" I ask Lucky as I walk into the kitchen. Picking up the bag of food, I fill up her bowl and carry the water bowl to the sink. Once both bowls are filled to the brim and I've given her my goodbye scrubs, I grab my keys and step out the door. Locking up behind me.

Looking in the window, I see Lucky's already laying on her big bed in the hallway. She maintains a strict schedule that involves pissing at five in the morning, eating three times a day, and bedtime by nine.

I hop on the back of my bike, rev her up, and ride down the drive and into the road.

There's an open spot right in front of KJ's and I take it happily.

Walking in, the jukebox is blasting and the regulars are in their seats. Chucking my chin up at everyone I pass, I make my way to the end of the bar where the guys already are. Beers in hand. "Hey! It's the birthday boy!" Wren yells over the crowd.

A loud chorus of cheers sounds from the entirety of the bar and I smile, waving my hand. I'm pretty sure my face is bright fucking red.

"Happy Birthday, Butch!" Surprised, I turn around to face Gemma. I haven't seen her around here in a long time.

"Hey!" I yell back over the noise, hugging her back. "You look good, Gemma."

And she does. She looks damn good. Her hair must be her natural color. It's not blonde, but it's light brown. She's got color in her cheeks, more skin on her bones, and she looks happy.

Smiling, she grabs a guy's arm that's standing next to her. "Thanks! I want you to meet my boyfriend, Doug."

"Nice to meet you," he says as I shake his hand. "I've heard a lot about you, Butch."

"Oh yeah?"

Smiling huge, Gemma leans into Doug's body. "I told him that you boys here in Eddington saved my life. And if it weren't for all of you, I never would have gone home. *And* if

I hadn't gone home," She says, smiling up at her boyfriend with puppy dog eyes, squeezing his waist, "Then I never would have met Doug."

"I think you're giving us a little too much credit, Gemma," Kurt chimes in. Standing next to me, he pats my shoulder. Going home was probably the best thing she could have done for herself. And Jax had told me, once Gemma filed the report with him the very next morning after Mitch beat the shit out of her, that it was Francine that had convinced her to come forward about him and go home. Now Mitch is sittin' pretty in county jail awaiting his trial on drug possession, drug sales, and domestic violence charges.

"It's true!" She yells over the music. "Anyway, Doug wanted to see the place I'm always talking about, so we decided to make the trip. Had no idea it was your birthday, Butch!"

"Yeah. Well, glad to see you. And today's just the same as any other day."

I break apart from the conversation with Gemma, her man, and Kurt and finish working my way to my stool. Wren and Jax both have a beer ready for me as soon as I sit down.

"Here's to another year!" Jax says, toasting my mug.

"And many more!" Wren adds right before we all take a deep swig.

I may not be big on birthdays, but if my friends insist on celebrating it, this is the best way to do it.

I don't stay out too late, and I don't drink too much since I've got to work tomorrow. I hang out for a while, order a burger, and have a good time with my buds before going home.

And when my head hits my pillow, and my dog covers my

feet, I smile. It's been a damn good birthday.

TWENTY-THREE
Hell, No

Things are quiet in the garage.

We brought a few tows into town earlier in the week, but the phone hasn't rung yet today.

I take the opportunity to clean up shop. It's a nice day, so I pull out the Firebird, give her a good bath, open all the sliding doors, and vacuum the shit out of the garage. Working up a sweat, I take off my shirt and tuck it into the back of my pants. I'm on my fifth bucket of clean water for mopping, enjoying the breeze that's cutting through the air, and listening to Creedence Clearwater Revival on the radio.

I don't hear her when she walks up behind me.

"So, this is the other girl you saved."

I stand straight, not sure if my head's playing tricks on me. It's not like I haven't woken up in the middle of the night countless times with her voice in my head. This could very well be my mind bringing more not funny jokes.

I turn around and sure as shit, there's Francine. Leaning against the Firebird parked right outside the open doors. She's wearing a white tank top, cut-off jean shorts, and a pair of white high top tennis shoes.

Her hair's curling wild around her head and the way she's

standing against my car, she looks like she's in a fucking MTV video.

I don't say anything. My tongue's too tied-up to try.

She pushes off my car, and starts to walk into the garage. Crossing her arms in front of her, she lowers her voice. "You said you loved me."

My eyes are on her every move as she approaches me. But I still can't talk. I don't know what the hell to say.

She stops just shy of arm's length from me. "Do you still, Butch?"

I take my time looking her over. She looks the exact same, but a thousand times better because she's right in front of me again. Right where I can reach out and touch her if I want to. And I sure as shit want to.

When I don't answer her question, her voice trembles, "Is it too late? Am I too late?"

"Hell, no." I drop the mop from my hands and grab her body, pulling it against mine. I don't know how or why she's here. I don't know what's happened since the day she walked out of my house and went to Clarks Grove and right now, I don't give a good god damn. All I care about is that she's standing here. In my garage. And she's close enough that I can smell her. Close enough to kiss her. So, I do. And I do it hard.

And when we finally come up for air, I'm wiping tears off her cheeks. "I'm so sorry Butch. God! I'm so sorry! I should never have believed - I should never have left. And then when you came, I wanted to leave with you! I did! But they had Lucy Lou! Keeping me from leaving by keeping her from me! I didn't - I didn't know what to do! I was scared! I'm so so so sorry!"

"Hey, hey! Shhhh," I tell her, holding her face in my hands and rememorizing every freckle that dots across her nose. "Where's Lou Lou now, Franny?" My mind already racing with how I can rally Wren, Jax, and Kurt here in less than five minutes to go get Lucy Lou out of that castle of horrors the Whitmore's call home.

Pulling her head back an inch, her brows lower in confusion. "She's with Gran!" She says, looking at me like I'm crazy for assuming she could possibly be anywhere else.

I bark out a laugh. "What?" She asks, her face serious.

Thinking I don't understand, she continues, "As soon as we had a way, I grabbed Lou Lou and left Magnolia Street. I called a cab and we went straight home. But you weren't there. Obviously, since it's a work day. The back door was locked and there was a dog barking inside, so I went over to Gran's. She confiscated Lou Lou from my arms before I even had a chance to go inside her house and threw me the keys to her car telling me to come to you. Here I am."

She throws her arms out as if to show me that she is in fact here. "And I'm not sure if I'll ever get Lou Lou back from Gran again. Is she mad at me?" But she doesn't stop to let me answer. "*And*, I'm not sure how I feel about a dog. Especially a big dog that will trip me up on walks. Lord knows I already trip enough on my own." She bites her bottom lip. "But Lou Lou will love it."

I stare at her for a full minute before everything she just said registers. And then I bust out laughing. And then I kiss her again for calling the house home. And then I bust a gut once more at her ticked off face.

"I fucking love you, Francine Whitmore."

Her eyes soften and she leans into me. "Well, that's good, Butch Casady. Because I love you, and I am never leaving you again."

"I wouldn't let you," I promise.

After making out a little more. Scratch that. After making out a lot more, I start cleaning up the garage and putting everything away so we can get out of here and get home. I'm anxious to see Lou Lou.

Laughing, Franny pulls her hand from mine, "Butch, I'm not going anywhere. You'd get things done a lot faster if you let go of me and use both hands!"

I reach out and grab her hand again. "I'm not riskin' it," I tell her with the stupid grin that's been on my face since she came back. Pulling her alongside me, listening to her giggle, I drop the empty bucket and mop where they go and flip the light switch off.

She follows me to the front as I check the door and she's right with me when I pull the last rolling door down. I lock it and squeeze her hand in mine. "You want to take the Firebird home?"

"I drove Gran's car, remember?"

"Yep. So, I drive the Oldsmobile and you drive the Firebird. Done."

She laughs incredulously. "You're going to let me drive your fancy car?"

"Darlin', what's mine is yours."

Wrapping her arms around my neck, she hugs me tight. "I know I don't have much, Franny, but I can give us a good life."

Her face is buried in my neck, "Stop, Butch. Just. Stop."

Raising her head, she rests her forehead against my lips and whispers, "I've had more with you than I've ever had in my life. Lou Lou, too."

Kissing that pretty head one more time, I rub her shoulders, "Let's go home, yeah?"

And we do. I follow my woman, driving my car, all the way home. And when she meets me at Gran's side door, I feel a moment of hesitancy. "What if she forgot me?" I ask Franny.

"I don't think that's possible, Butch." She answers quietly. "But, if she did, it'll only be temporary."

I steel myself up, take a big gulp of air, and open the door. Either way, I've got to man up and find out.

There's a whole lot of laughing going on in the family room. And when we stop in the doorway between the kitchen and where Bobby, Gran, and Lou Lou are playing on the floor, I see why.

Bobby's wearing a dress hat and scarf, serving a miniature cup of pretend tea to Granny Jean and Lucy Lou. They don't notice us watching at first, and Francine is covering her mouth with her hand so they don't hear her laughing and ruin the moment.

And when Lucy Lou's eyes look up and meet mine, I feel frozen in time.

"Dada!" She squeals, pushing her little hands against the soft brown carpet she's sitting on and running over to me. Her arms are flailing and her hair is bouncing, and I am happy as a damn clam.

I kneel down, my ass on my heels and throw my arms out to catch her. "There's my girl!"

Unbending my body, I stand straight, holding Lou Lou tight, and look at Francine. All is right in my world.

"You want to meet the puppy, Lou Lou?"

"Puppy!" The pink princess in my arms shrieks in excitement, clapping her hands.

"Oh goodness," Francine exclaims under her breath.

Chuckling, I look at her, "You'll love her, sweetheart."

Picking up that we're about to leave, Granny comes over and hugs Francine. "I'm glad you're both back where you're supposed to be."

"Me too," Francine says through more tears.

"Darlin', you have got to stop crying," I tell her, taking Lucy Lou to the door.

"Poppycock. Don't listen to him. The only time men get feelings is when they're feelin' thirsty," Granny Jean says.

Bobby and I both yell out at the same time, "I heard that!"

"Speaking of which, I think pizza and beer sounds great for dinner. Gran, Bob, you in?"

Coming into the kitchen from the family room, Bobby stands behind Granny with his hand on her shoulder.

"Not tonight, Butch. You enjoy dinner with your girls. We'll do dinner soon." Grabbing Francine's hand, she adds with a wink, "If you need a sitter tonight, just bring her on over."

We say our goodbyes and walk next door.

And holding Lucy Lou up a little higher, I unlock the back door, and introduce everyone. "Girls, this crazy barking fluffball is Lucky. Lucky, this is your mom and your sister."

"PUPPY!" Lucy Lou screams, kicking her feet to get down and get her tiny hands on the dog.

Raising my brows, I turn my head to Franny and wait for her permission.

She's already lowered herself down to the floor. And as soon as she's on her ass, her porcelain-colored skin gets lost in the sea of black hair. She's laughing and getting a load of drool-laced kisses on her face. "Lou Lou! Come get some puppy smooches!"

The little white tennis shoes aren't on the kitchen floor for one second before Lucy Lou launches herself into the Francine and Lucky fiasco.

I sit my ass on the floor, too. And on the floor, right in front of the door, is where we stay for the better part of an hour. Until finally, Lucky tuckers out on her bed and Lucy Lou disappears into the family room in search of her toys that are all still there.

"She's a good dog, Butch. And I love her name," Francine scooches over to me and I spread my legs and rest against the door so she can lay back on me.

Rubbing her arms, I agree. "Yeah, she's great."

"Do you want Gran to watch Lou Lou tonight?" She twists her neck so she can look up at me.

I know my answer straight away. "Nope. Tomorrow you might as well plan on being naked all day because I'm callin' off work and you're not leaving my bed. But tonight, I want to go to sleep with all my girls under my roof. Right where they should be. At home.

"Kissing my chin, she settles back against my chest. "God, I love you," she sighs.

TWENTY-FOUR
I Am. I Do. And Yes.

Licking my way up Francine's thigh, I taste a salty sweet mix of her and me on my tongue.

Instead of digging in, I tease her, licking the crease of her thigh and running my nose across her pussy to lick the other side.

She grabs my hair and tugs hard in frustration. I snigger and blow air across her slit.

"Butch..." She moans with her eyes closed tight. I give in and take her there, my tongue works hard and fast. Her soft, wet skin skates across the front of my teeth as I worship her pussy until she comes.

Once she's sedated, I crawl up the bed and over her body, kissing every few inches along the trip.

When I make it to the top, I give her a long, wet kiss, covering her face in everything that's covering mine, and I drop over at her side. My head lands hard on the bed, and my arm is draped across her breasts.

"I can't move," she laughs out of breath.

I grunt into the pillow.

As soon as we woke up this morning, I dropped Lucy Lou off at Gran's and practically ran across the lawns to my house after telling Francine she'd better be naked and ready by the time I got back. She was magnificently nude, as requested, and we've both been insatiable with one another's body ever since.

I palm her breast. "Tell me about where you've been."

I can feel her chest rise and fall with a heavy sigh. We both knew this conversation was coming. And for as much as I'd love to just start shit off right where we left it, there's a lot of in-between that needs to be filled in. For the both of us.

"Well," she starts and stops. "I guess I should start at the beginning. When I left."

She laces her fingers through the hand that had been cupping her breast. An anchor that we probably both need. "Not long after you dropped me off that day, Lucy Lou and I were in the family room, and someone was knocking on the front door. When I opened the door, I was surprised to see that it was one of my father's men. I recognized him from Magnolia Street. He handed me the packet of papers and said he'd be waiting outside to take us home. He told me not to take too long."

She laughs quietly, "He and my father were so sure that I'd leave. And I was such a fool that I did. I looked through the records, saw the pictures, and let all of my fears and insecurities from growing up in a home with no love and the years I wasted with Stephen get to me. My father knew just what to show me to make me believe that you had used me. That you were only with me for the money. And as soon as I was secure and back inside Magnolia Street, back in his clutches, I was placed under a strict lock and key. Eyes on me all the time. I couldn't get to a phone. I wasn't permitted to leave. I couldn't even see Lou Lou unless the "visitation" was approved by my father. She was with a nanny all day and night. It was a prison and I was just a pawn in his game. And when I heard your voice in my father's office," her words crack and I can feel her breathing grow unsteady under my hand. "I almost screamed your name. I ran to the steps and had to stand there, watching you leave, wanting nothing more than to go with you. To beg you to save us. But what right did I have to ask that? You had already saved us. Twice. And I still turned my back on you and left. But God, Butch. When I heard you yell that you loved me? I knew. I *knew* that I would do whatever it would take to get us back to you. So, I bided my time. I memorized house staff schedules and played my part of the sorry, dutiful daughter committed to righting her wrongs. I was careful to hide any emotion throughout the day, and when I was alone in my room, I cried myself to sleep. Praying that you'd wait for us. That somehow, you would know that we were coming back."

Francine takes another full, deep breath. "My father had set up a docket of meetings with proper 'suitors.' It was determined that I would be publicly engaged by the end of the month. One of the men, the one I was to meet with yesterday, had insisted on meeting Lucy Lou as well. Some rich foreign banker. I'm assuming he wanted to see how well-behaved she was, or how easily it would be to pass her off as his own."

This has me lifting my head and grinding my teeth. That fucker was going to sell my woman off to the highest bidder. And the pure rage I feel at anyone "assessing" Lou Lou has me squeezing the pillow under my head.

"I knew that was our chance. So, I packed as much as I could in Lou Lou's diaper bag, and dressed in day clothes under my 'appropriate' attire. Downtown Clarks Grove is always busy and crowded and the parking is atrocious. Knowing we'd have to be dropped off a few blocks from the restaurant, I was relieved when we were even farther away than I had hoped. And as soon as we were out of the car, and out of sight of our driver, I slipped into an office building, tore off the ridiculous dress I was wearing, dug out my tennis shoes from the bottom of the bag, and left out the back entrance. We stopped at the first payphone I could find, called a cab, and we came home."

Instead of pointing out all of the fucking things that could have gone wrong with her plan, or the simple fact that she should have called *me* at the payphone instead of a damn cab, I take a few of my own deep breaths.

"If I had known, I'd have gotten you out of there, Francine." Referring to the afternoon that I was thrown out on my ass. I would have fought harder. "You and Lou Lou. Not a damn thing could have kept me from it."

I scratch my morning stubble. I guess it's my turn to talk. "Your father had tried to pay me off. Not just that day at the diner, but after you left. He sent me a hefty check and demanded I sign off that I'd never known you. And that I'd never come near either of you again. Threatened me and Wren. Swore he'd run us out of business. Obviously, I didn't sign 'em. Instead, I rode my bike out there and gave his fucking legal papers right back, along with his dirty money, and made it clear I wasn't putting my name on shit. Not until I saw you. Not until I knew that it was what you wanted."

"I would never have wanted that," she whispers, rolling her body over so we were facing each other.

"I know. Somehow, I knew that."

We lay there just staring at each other for a beat before she asks, "Did you wait for me? I mean, I know I left. And I know you don't even owe me an explanation. I don't even know if I have a right to ask. But," taking a deep breath, "did you find comfort with anyone else?" She may sound hesitant and simply inquisitive, but we both know that's a loaded question. And if I had rolled around in the sheets with someone while she was gone, was it really considered cheating since she'd left me?

"I did." I answer back honestly, and watch her not even try to mask her hurt. "I did wait for you, Franny. I didn't find comfort with any other woman other than the times I ate Granny's chocolate chip cookies or the nights I shoved my feet under Lucky's warm body before falling asleep." My fingers brush a lock of her hair behind her ear. "I wouldn't have been able to touch anyone else without thinking of you the whole time."

The air of relief that escapes her mouth is loud, and she closes her eyes tight. "I would have understood. I promised myself every time I thought about it that I would understand if you did. *Why* you did. But, I ... I don't know..."

I can't help but laugh a little at her confession. "Darlin', if I'd found out you'd been in someone else's pants while you were gone from me, I'd have lost my shit."

Smiling, she opens her eyes back up and moves her head closer to mine. We kiss. And then we fall fast asleep wrapped up in a tangle of skin and limbs. We have a lot more to talk about. But, that's more than enough for now.

Waking up later, I stretch and reach out for Franny. When my hand touches nothing but cold sheets, I start to panic until I take in the sound of dishes clanging downstairs and the smell of bacon hitting my nose. Rolling over, I look at the red numbers on the digital clock sitting on the bed stand. It's four in the afternoon.

The jeans are closer than the boxer shorts, so I put them on commando, not bothering with the button. On my way down, I notice Lucky isn't following me down the way she normally does. And when I get to the kitchen, I see why.

My woman's at the stove, flipping bacon with a fork in one of my old shirts, and Lucky's sitting pretty at her feet. "Sweetheart, it's dinnertime, not breakfast."

She looks up and smiles huge at me. Those baby blues glowing. "Yeah, well, you don't have anything in the fridge except beer, old chicken wings, and bacon."

"That's true." I step behind her and wrap my hands around her small waist, resting my chin on her shoulder so I can watch her cook. "I missed your food."

"I missed cooking *for* you. You and Lou Lou both. I forgot how portion controlled, and well, just *controlled*, our meals were on Magnolia Street."

Lucky hasn't moved since I walked in. No hi dad. Nothing. "Traitor," I mutter to her furry face.

Giggling, a sweet sound I have missed sorely, Francine slaps one of the hands I have clasped in front of her. "Don't talk to her like that!"

I grab one of the crisp pieces sitting on the napkin covered plate off to the side, and shove it in my mouth. "What do you want to do tomorrow?"

"What do I want to do tomorrow?" She laughs, "Butch, you have to work!"

I swallow what's in my mouth. "Nah. I was thinking we'd get married instead."

She drops the fork right in the popping grease. "What?"

I reach over and turn the stove knob to the off position and I slide the sizzling pan off the hot coils. Pulling her into me, I repeat myself. "I said, let's get married."

"Are you ... do you ... really?" She's blinking and stuttering and it's damn cute.

"I am. I do. And yes." I answer all her half questions. "If we're doing this Francine, we're doing this all the way."

She scrutinizes me for a half second before leaning into me, rocking us both back, "Okay," she whispers, "Let's do it."

"Good." I kiss her hard and quick and slap her ass. "I'm going to go get dressed and run out. I'll be back in a bit. You'll bring Lou Lou back home, yeah?"

Calling after me, she asks, "Out? Where are you going?"

I'm already at the steps when I stop and look back at her standing in my kitchen. Wearing my clothes. My dog at her feet. "Gotta get the ring darlin'. And food. After everything we just did upstairs, I'm gonna need more than bacon."

The sound of her giggling follows me up the steps, and I smile like a fool the entire time I'm dressing.

TWENTY-FIVE
SHE'S MY WIFE

We've been standing here in the Eddington County City Hall for ten minutes, and I haven't heard a damn thing the Mayor has said.

All I know is that Franny's standing in front of me - looking like fucking goddess in her white dress and her hair pinned up with those unruly curls falling down her face and neck - my family is behind me - Gran and Bobby, Wren, Jax and Kurt - and Lou Lou is between us - also in all white and damn adorable. And after Mayor Beck finishes saying all the shit he's saying, Franny will be my wife.

When I ran over to Gran's last night to get my mother's wedding ring she'd kept safe for me all these years, I thought Gran was going to have a heart attack. The woman was jumping up and down, clapping, crying, and yelling. It was quite a show. And she was up first thing this morning, waiting for the doors of Montgomery Ward to open so she could buy Franny and Lou Lou white dresses.

And when I stopped at KJ's to pick up after-hours-of-sex-food and tell the boys the news, we had a celebratory beer, and they all three said they'd be there, like I knew they would.

But what I wasn't expecting was for Franny to make a few plans of her own while I was gone, and get Bobby to pick up a shit ton of red carnations from all the florists around Eddington to use for her bouquet and to decorate City Hall with.

She even ordered a cake from the grocery store- something I never would have thought to do.

Now, here we are. And I can't stop thinking that twenty-four hours ago, I woke up alone with a hole the size of a crater in my heart, and this morning I woke up next to my soulmate, listening to my little girl scream for me from the room next door. Life can be fucking funny sometimes.

"Butch?" Mayor Beck says my name, reprimanding me for not listening.

"Hm?" I answer, breaking my stare from Franny over to where he's standing on the step just above where the two of us are standing, facing each other. I swear he's in the same suit and tie he's worn every day for the past 37 years. His balding head is shining under the fluorescent lights above us and his spectacles are thicker than glass block windows.

He clears his throat and looks down, peering under his glasses, at the old, tattered book in his hands, and speaks louder. "I asked, if you take Francine Whitmore to be your lawfully wedded wife, to have, and to hold -"

"Yep." I break in, cutting him off.

The boys are chuckling behind me and Franny's shaking her head at me, smiling.

"What about you, Franny?" I ask, tucking a stray curl behind her ear.

"Yes, Butch. I do." She replies, her beautiful eyes glowing.

I wrap my hand around her neck and pull her forward, Lou Lou standing between us playing with the flower pots full of red blooms all around on the floor. I kiss my wife long and slow.

"Well, that's not how it goes," Mayor Beck mutters, his finger pushing his glasses up his nose. We ignore him, enjoying our kiss as husband and wife, and I hear his book slam closed and his exasperated sigh.

"Nah," my voice quiet, my beautiful woman all I can see. "I think that's exactly how it goes."

The boys start hootin' and hollerin' and pull Franny from me, each of them taking a turn to hug and kiss her. I can hear the shudder of Bobby's camera capturing it all. Granny grabs my arm to turn me around and hug me tight, tears in her eyes. "I'm so happy, Butch."

"Me too, Gran." I kiss her cheek.

"I should have bought you dress pants, too," she admonishes, pulling away and looking down at my blue jeans.

"Nah. I wouldn't have worn 'em anyway," I smirk.

Bobby walks up to us, snaps a picture, and says, "Congratulations, Butch. I don't know how you landed such a high-class lady, but you sure won the lottery with that one." He shakes my hand.

"You have no idea," I say as I stand off to the side and watch Franny laugh and joke with the boys as they tickle and toss Lou Lou around.

Kurt yells out that it's time for a round of drinks and a slice of cake back at the pub; everyone shouts out in agreement. And when we walk out, everyone grabs a pot of carnations or two to put in the back of my truck.

Pulling in front of the bar, I look like I'm some flower delivery guy or some shit with the back of my ride spilling over with flowers. Looking through the back window, thinking the same thing as me, Francine laughs. "Maybe I ordered too many."

"Nope." I answer, looking right at her. "You did good."

"Let's go eat our wedding cake, husband," she says, smiling huge.

"Yep," I answer, right before I kiss her long and good. "I like the sound of that on your lips, wife." I admit, squeezing her neck one more time before hopping out and opening her door for her.

The little white sandals on her feet don't hit the pavement, because I lift her in my arms. "Butch!" She giggles, "You're supposed to carry me inside of the house. Not inside of a bar!"

"I'll carry you anywhere you want, darlin'."

She reaches out and pulls open the old wood door for me, just enough that I can finish opening it with my foot.

Everyone shouts and celebrates when we walk in and even Jimmy from the local paper, the Eddington Express, has shown up to take a picture. "We're starting a new section on local weddings." He tells me after he snaps a picture of Franny in my arms. "My grandmother told me all about the shotgun wedding this morning and thought I'd take a few shots. Is that okay with you two?"

Jimmy's grandmother is friends with mine, so no doubt Granny was busy on the phone all last night. "No problem Jimmy." I answer, feeling real happy-go-lucky and not giving a damn about anything.

Passing by a bunch of people clapping and congratulating, I carry Franny to her seat and kiss her cheek before setting her down next to where Gran's sitting with Lou Lou in her lap.

"Mama!" Lucy says, hands out to be picked up.

"Hey, baby," Franny coos, taking Lucy Lou and kissing her cheek. My chest fills with pride watching *my* girls sitting together.

Kurt walks up behind the bar and slaps his hand down on the bar. "Who wants cake?"

"ME!" Screams Lucy, raising her hands into the air. We all laugh and Kurt promises her the first piece.

We spent a few hours talking, eating cake, drinking beer (well, Franny drank her wine), and now I'm holding my woman, slow dancing to Bryan Adams singing about Heaven.

"This is definitely my version of Heaven," I whisper to Francine.

She's resting her head against my chest. Lifting it up, her face close to mine, she says, "I'm so glad I found you, Butch."

"Darlin', you didn't just find me. You found home."

Sighing, she rests her head back against me and repeats what I said. "I found home."

"Speaking of which," I turn her in my arms quickly and dip her back, "What do you say we head home?" I waggle my eyes in suggestion.

Laughing, she lets me pull her back up. "Okay, Butch. Take me home."

I waste no time tellin' everyone we're heading out, and I practically have to carry Franny out because she's taking so long with her hugs and goodbyes.

The last stop on our way out is Gran and Lucy Lou. They're having one of their sleepovers tonight. "See you tomorrow kid," I tell Lou Lou, picking her up and giving her a hug. I hand her off to Franny to do the same, and then I'm dragging her out the door and back into my truck.

When we get to the house, I carry Franny through the back door and put her down in the kitchen. It's starting to get dark and Lucky's been stuck inside all day while we were out doing shit like getting married.

I kiss Francine real quick and grab the leash hanging by the door. "You get ready. I'm gonna take Luck out for a quick walk. And what I mean by ready, is naked."

"Oh! I want to go on a walk, too!" She pouts, petting Lucky and giving her kisses all over her dark hairy head.

Powerless to tell her no, I wait for Franny to change into what she calls her "day clothes" which are really just "any time clothes."

Coming into the kitchen in a pair of jeans and a white shirt, her hair still pinned up on top of her head, I whistle. "Damn. You're the only lady I've ever met that looks that good getting ready to take the dog for a walk."

Franny rolls her eyes, feigning irritation. "You always think I look good, Butch Casady."

Clipping the leash onto Lucky's collar, I answer, "I sure do *Francine Casady.*"

"Alright, woman. Let's get this over with. I have plans for us tonight." I tell her, opening the door and waiting for her to pass by.

TWENTY-SIX
MY DOG

I make sure we take a quick walk, but it's still fully dark by the time we make it back home.

Francine has Lucky's leash in her hands and she's just given me a hard time for rushing around the block. "It's not like we haven't slept together before, Butch." She had teased, bumping her shoulder into mine.

"Darlin', this is the first time I'll be sleeping with my *wife* and I intend to get that started in less than ten minutes." I answered seriously.

Now they're jogging ahead of me and up the driveway. Francine is laughing as they race each other, promising Lucky a biscuit as they round the corner towards the back door. I stop at the mailbox in the road and am just closing the door of the white box with a couple envelopes in my hand when I hear a loud popping sound coming from behind my house.

Recognizing the sound, but not understanding it, I drop what's in my hands and run fast down the cement. I can hear Lucky barking and growling aggressively in a way I've never heard her do before.

Not thinking to flip on the security light above the door

before we left, it's pitch black back here. And when I skid around the corner, my heart beating wildly, the first thing I see is Lucky viciously biting a guy's arm and something black dropping from his fingers and onto the ground. He's screaming and Lucky's pulling him down to the ground with her jaw locked on his arm.

But when I make out Francine's white shoes glowing bright in the dark, spread apart and facing up because she's laid out on her back half on the stoop and half on the brick patio, I lose my fucking mind.

Running to her, I gently pick up her head in my hands. I'm screaming her name and she slowly opens up her eyes. Trying to see where she's hurt is hard as fuck because it's so damn fucking dark back here. "I think I'm okay," she answers. Confusion on her face and in her weak voice.

Gran's backlight turns on, illuminating us a little bit. "Butch!" She screams from the door. "What's going on back here?"

"Go inside and call the police! Now!" I yell back over Lucky's incessant snarling and barking. Gran's screaming and the sound of her back door slamming behind her echoes between our backyards.

"Where are you hurt?" I ask, absolutely panicked as I try to look at and touch every inch of her.

She pushes up on her hands to try to sit up. "My head hurts," she winces, trying to lift her arm to her head. That's when I see the red, wet and dripping down her arm and all over her side. Her white shirt is soaked through with it.

I can hear someone running over and I see the beam of a flashlight in the corner of my eye. "Butch, there's somebody over here!"

It's Bobby, out of breath, standing between where I'm holding my wife and where someone is lying in my grass. Bobby's flashlight is aimed at where Lucky's paws are pressing down against his chest with her hackles raised. That fucker's a dead man, but right now, all I can concentrate on is my wife.

"I think you were shot, darlin'," I tell Francine, picking her up just enough to be able to slide her back so she can rest against the door on the stoop.

"I can't feel my arm," she whispers to me. Her face ghostly pale in the weak light coming from next door.

I hear the sirens coming down my street and I almost pass out from relief. "I know, baby. We're gonna get you all sorted out here real soon," I promise. Even though they came quick, it still feels like they took fucking forever to get here.

"Hands on your head, fucker!" Jax's angry voice is behind me but my eyes don't leave Francine's. "Just look at me, darlin'," I tell her gently to keep her from worrying about anything else but her.

The flashing lights bouncing off my garage let me know the ambulance made it to the drive, and not two seconds later, two guys in dark shirts come around the corner of the house.

"What do we got?" One asks me, kneeling down next to me and Franny.

"She's been shot. In the arm. I think that's it, but she says her head hurts." My voice is shaky as hell.

I'm still holding her hand, but I move over to make more room for the guy to do a quick scan of her body and her arm.

Please, don't let there be any more gunshot wounds.

The voices, beeps, and static from Jax's police transceiver add to the chaos going on around me. He's calling for back-up, the sirens are blaring, and Lucky's not letting up on her barking.

"Alright, ma'am. It looks like it's just your arm. Your heads got a good gash, but that's probably from when you fell. My buddy's going to grab the stretcher and we're going to get you to the hospital and get you all patched up, okay?"

"Okay," Francine says so quietly I think I'm the only one that heard.

"What's her name, Butch?" The paramedic recognizes me, but I have no clue who the hell he is. There's just too fucking much going on right now. I just look at him with a blank look on my face so he asks me again.

"Uh, Francine. Francine Casady. She's my wife."

"Okay. We've only got room for us in the truck. You'll have to meet us at the hospital." Squeaky wheels from the stretcher scratch against the cement. The other guy locks the wheels and comes around to Francine's other side, forcing me to let go of her hand.

"On three," he says to the first guy.

I watch them pick up my wife and set her down slowly on the stretcher. Once she's fully laid out, they're buckling the straps across her body. "Franny," I say, following them as they roll her down my driveway, "Franny, I'll be right behind you!"

They lift the stretcher, the front wheels fold in and they push the bed all the way in. One of the guys is running around to jump into the driver's seat, the other is quickly slamming the backdoor, blocking me from seeing Francine. The box truck is backing up, away from me, and the sound of sirens crack my eardrum as they speed away.

"Butch!" I can hear Jax screaming for me, yelling my name, but I can't move. "Dammit Butch! Fucking wake up!"

I blink a few times and turn around. Jax is aiming his gun to the ground, Bobby's standing off to the side, his flashlight still trained on whoever's on the ground. And Lucky's still losing her shit.

"We can't get near him without her trying to rip our arm off! You've got to come get Lucky!" Jax is screaming, not moving his eyes from his target.

Every fucking thing that has happened since I stopped to get my mail slams into me all at once. The gunshots, the barking, the screaming, the sirens, the ambulance - all of it.

And I'm stalking towards the man that just tried to kill my wife.

"Lucky! Go!" I command, my dog listening immediately and backing off the man on the ground.

My foot makes contact with the gun he used, sending it flying across the grass as lean over him and grab his dark shirt at his chest, pulling the fucker forward and off the ground. I rear back in recognition.

There's blood on his face from the fresh bite mark on his neck courtesy of my dog. "It wasn't supposed to be her. It.. .it...it wasn't supposed to be her." He's stuttering, repeating himself.

"Yeah. Well, motherfucker, it *was* her," Jax seethes. I can feel Jax's hand and gun getting closer to his head.

"You're supposed to be in jail," Jax says darkly.

"I'm guessing Daddy Whitmore posted bail," I answer for Stephen Black between my teeth.

"I'm so dead," Stephen cries. "I was supposed to take care of you." He says pointedly to me. "That was the deal. Now he's gonna kill me. I'm so dead," he cries again.

"Yeah, you are," my fist connecting with his cheek. Over and over again I hit him. The satisfying crack of bone and skin under my knuckles is the only thing I can feel. His blood splattering all over him the only thing I can see.

My arms are in a hold and are being pulled back. I'm fighting against it, trying to get back to the son of a bitch that shot my wife.

"Butch, it's okay. She's okay." I hear someone chanting in my ear.

I watch as Jax cuffs Stephen and pulls him up to his feet roughly. Grabbing him by the crook of his arm, Jax starts pushing him down my driveway towards his cruiser. He looks up at whoever's with me, "Get him to her."

"Come on man, let's go to the hospital," a familiar voice says to me.

Turning my neck to see who's touching me, my head in a fog, I take in Wren and Kurt each holding an arm to keep me from following Jax and finishing what I started with Stephen's face.

I look past them and back to where Francine had been on the stoop. The cement stained red where she'd fallen.

"My dog..." I mumble.

"I got her Butch," Bobby answers. "And Jean's got Lou Lou. We're fine here. You go on with the boys." Lucky is sitting calmly at his feet. Totally relaxed and panting, her big

229

pink tongue hanging out of her mouth, like she didn't just maul the Hell out of a grown man.

TWENTY-SEVEN
Hell, Yes

Holding Francine's hand, I rest my arms on the hospital bed and watch her sleep.

She's hooked up to all kinds of shit and the machines are beeping all around us. Wren and Kurt left a while ago once they were sure Francine was going to be okay and that I wasn't going to lose my shit and run off looking for Stephen Black.

There's a knock on the door and it cracks open. "She wake up, yet?" Jax asks quietly, poking his head in.

I shake my head no.

Coming all the way in, he pockets his hands into his blue uniform pants. "Doctor said she'll be up soon."

I lower my head and rub my hand across the back of my neck. "I didn't want her to go on the walk. If she'd have stayed home, it would have been me. It *should* have been me."

"It's not your fault, Butch. And you know it. You wanna be pissed off at someone, be pissed off at Richard Whitmore."

"SOB posted bail for Stephen this morning. Sounds like as soon as he found out Fran managed to escape from underneath him, he figured out exactly where she went and arranged Stephen's 'get out of jail free' card with the agreement that he'd handle you immediately. Stephen came to Eddington and waited 'til you came home. Unfortunately, he was high as a kite by the time he stumbled into your backyard and mistook Fran for you. But even more unfortunate for him, Lucky was there and wasn't havin' any of it. According to Stephen, Lucky attacked him right before he got the shot out. Causing him to miss the intended target of her back and knick her arm instead. And to be honest, after seeing Stephen in the bright lights of the hospital, I'd say he got off worse than everyone. And not just because of the professional facial treatment you gave him, but also because of the scars he'll carry on his hand, arm, and neck from Lucky's jaw."

Jax grunts and adds, "Well, I suppose his forever may not be that long if Richard manages to get to him first."

I rub my eyes and look at the bandages wrapped around Francine's head and arm. "This is all so fucking crazy."

"Yep," Jax answers. "And you're going to need to prepare Fran for the firestorm that's coming."

"What?" No clue what the hell he's talking about.

"Butch, the daughter of the international banking institution, Whitmore House, was just shot. On the same day she got hitched at City Hall to a not-wealthy towing company operator in Eddington. The hitman - her ex - who also happens to be a drug-dealing thief and the father of her child - born out of wedlock - was conveniently released from prison on bond this morning. *And,* he went on record saying he was hired by Richard Whitmore himself to kill his ex's new husband. This is going to be a media shitstorm. And you and Fran are going to be smackdab in the middle of it."

"Fuck."

"Yeah," Jax agrees. "So, we need to prepare. And come up with a plan to minimize Fran and Lou Lou's exposure. Judy's already called me from the office saying faxes are coming in requesting statements from newspapers in Clarks Grove. Word is spreading fast. My suggestion is that you close up shop at the garage and you guys lay low at home for the next few days. They're going to want to trail you, your employees, your grandmother, and your wife. And they're going to be desperate for a comment. I can have my guys sit out front of the house and keep the news trucks away. After a few days of nothing, I imagine they'll give up and go away."

"Done." I answer. Thankful for friends in high places.

"I'll do what I can when she's released and you leave the hospital, but they're still going to be here, Butch."

I nod. "I guess we'll figure that out when it comes."

"I'm heading out, unless you need anything before I go?"

"No." I say, looking back down at Francine.

He turns around and starts walking out but I stop him. "Thanks, Jax. For everything."

"Anytime." He tips his chin towards Francine. "She's one of us now. We protect our family."

Jax closes the door quietly behind him and I reach over to switch off the light above Francine's head. Sitting back in the uncomfortable chair, I settle in for a long night. There's no way I can calm down enough to rest. Not until Francine's eyes are open, I've seen her up and moving, all this tubing shit isn't connected to her anymore, and we're lying together in our bed.

Honestly, after a few hours of nurses coming in and out, voices over the speaker in the hallway, and the harping of the medical equipment in the room, I don't know how in the hell anyone can sleep in a hospital.

Another nurse just walked out after checking all the papers printing out different colored jagged lines, and I feel Francine's fingers wiggle against my palm.

"Hey darlin'," I whisper. Sitting up a bit farther so I can get closer to her face.

"Hey," she scratches back. Her throat sounds dry.

"You want some water?"

Franny nods her head, and I reach over to push the button that raises half the bed up at an incline.

Once she's sitting up, I lift the pink jug full of ice water off the bedside table and hold the straw up to her mouth. She sucks a few good gulps of the cold water down her throat before laying her head back against her pillow.

"How you feelin' sweetheart?"

A small grin pulls up her lips. "Great."

I smile back. "I think you're lying."

"How bad is it?" She asks.

"Not too bad, really. You have a good knot on your head due to hitting the concrete. That had to be sewn closed, and they're watching you for a day."

She looks down at her arm. "And this?"

"That," I answer angrily, "Is a failed attempt your father made at me."

Closing her eyes, she takes a deep breath. "I'm sorry, Butch."

"What the hell for?"

"For this. For everything I've put you through. For everything you've had to do for us." Francine opens her eyes and pins them on me. "I'm sure your life would have been a lot less dramatic had I never come back."

"I'm only going to say this once, Francine Casady. So, listen up." I stand so I can lean over the top half of her body. My hands push down on the hard mattress on either side of her small form. "You are mine. You were meant to be mine. Otherwise, we never would have crossed paths at Quick Mart in the middle of the night. And you will not now, *or ever*, take responsibility for the decisions your bastard father has made."

She breathes in deep, and reaches out slowly towards my chest. I look down to her hands grabbing a handful of my white shirt and slide my eyes back up to watch her face get closer to mine because she's pulling me in.

"Kiss me," she breathes against my mouth.

And I do. Nice and slow and long. Putting every ounce of relief I feel that she's okay and in my arms into the kiss.

When I finish, I lean farther over, and pick up the phone. I pound in the numbers written across the top so I can call outside the hospital and then pound in Gran's number.

Straightening up, but still leaning over Francine, I wait for Granny to pick up.

"Hello?" She answers, anxious and clearly hoping it's me.

"She's fine," I say into the phone with my eyes locked on Francine's. "She's got a knot on her head from falling and a graze on her arm from the missed bullet. They're keeping her overnight to keep an eye on her head, but we'll be home sometime tomorrow."

"Oh, thank God!" Granny Jean exclaims. "My phone's been ringing off the hook with my friends checking in. But I kept the line clear waiting for you to call!"

"Lou Lou sleeping?" I ask, knowing that Franny wants to know.

"Yes. Little angel slept through the whole thing. She has no idea anything even happened," Gran says. "And you better believe I fed that dog some prime rib tonight. As far as I'm concerned, she deserves a cut of steak every night for the rest of her life!"

Franny can hear Gran since she's talking so loud into the phone and we both chuckle.

"Now who spoils her?" I ask Gran, teasing her.

Not that I'm arguing. Lucky's going to be living the high life from here on out. Not that she wasn't already, but even more so since she saved my woman's life.

"Poppycock!" Gran admonishes before I laugh and tell her goodbye. "Give Lou Lou a big kiss from us when she wakes up and tell her we'll be home soon."

Hanging up the phone, I pick up the remote. "Want to watch some tv?"

"Only if you can find Dallas," Franny answers.

I groan. "It's going to take a while to get used to having to watch girly shit."

"Aw. Poor baby." She scoots her body over as far as she can and pats the mattress. "Would you feel better if I held you while we watched it?"

"Hell yes," I say, taking off my dirty shirt and throwing it on the chair my ass has been plastered in for hours.

Situating myself next to her, we don't find Dallas on the tube, but we settle on an episode of Knots Landing instead.

It's just as bad as I thought it would be and I don't mind in the slightest.

TWENTY-EIGHT
I'D RISK IT

On the front of this week's Eddington Express is a huge black and white picture of me and Franny.

It was from the day we got married. That kid, Jimmy, took the shot for the wedding section of the paper. Francine is smiling huge and looking up at me. I may not be smiling, but I'm holding my wife in her white dress and looking down at her. And I remember exactly what I was thinking at that moment - that I was the luckiest damn man in the world.

But our wedding announcement isn't the reason the picture's the feature story. It's an entire damn four-page story about Eddington's newest resident. How her father raised his banking house empire into an international institution and how that institution gloriously, and publicly, fell due to corruption, power, and greed.

Francine had clipped the picture of the two of us out and put it on the front of the fridge with a few magnets, stating it was our official wedding picture- even though we had a ton of shots taken by Bobby.

And, if you turn to page 13 in the paper, you'll find a much smaller black and white picture of Richard Whitmore's mugshot.

According to the story, one day after Francine Whitmore, now Francine Casady, was shot by a Stephen Black, Richard Whitmore was arrested by a Chief Jax Finn of the Eddington Police Department on charges of aiding and abetting in attempted murder. Mr. Whitmore was later charged on several other counts of tax fraud and evasion by the United States government, as well as a long list of a whole bunch of other shit I don't understand and don't care about. Because the point is, the man's going to spend the rest of his life behind bars. Right next to that fucker Stephen Black.

Jax kept his word and had his men patrolling both mine and granny's house for the entire week after Franny was released from the hospital. And other than a couple reporters that were able to snap a few shitty, grainy shots from a distance in the parking lot of Eddington General, we stayed out of the national news.

Having become so loved by everyone in her short time here, the residents of our small town thoroughly and quickly ran the paparazzi right over the county line on behalf of Franny.

"Ready?" Franny asks me as she walks into the kitchen. Her candy smell fills the air, and I put down the paper I've read a dozen times already.

She's holding Lucy Lou on her side and they're both wearing matching pink polka-dot bikinis and pink sunglasses.

"My daughter's not wearing a bikini," I say, crossing my arms.

Francine puts Lucy Lou down on her feet and faces me, crossing her own arms. Her pink nails are wrapped around her bicep. "It's the only swimsuit she has."

"Then wrap her in a bag, for all I care. But she's not going out looking like that." My chin knocks in Lou Lou's direction. She's on the floor singing a song she learned at story time as she digs through her plastic basket of water toys next to Lucky's bed. The dog is just sitting patiently, wagging her tail, and waiting to leave.

Uncrossing her arms, Francine slides up to me with her bedroom eyes. She glides her hands up my t-shirt and around my neck. "I don't think any of the little boys at the community pool are going to notice her swimsuit." I can tell she's holding in laughter. "I think, for this year, she's safe from wandering eyes at the park."

The woman knows I can't fight her. Especially when she's wearing what she's wearing and looking at me like she's looking at me.

"And what about you?" I ask, my arms still crossed in front of me. "I'm pretty sure all the *big* boys are going to notice your swimsuit." My eyes veer down to the breasts pushed together in the skimpy fabric.

She finally lets out the laugh. "Do you think anyone is foolish enough to look at me when you're around?"

I raise my brows in answer. If she wasn't mine, you bet your ass I'd be foolish enough to look my fill at *all* of her if she showed up where I was wearing this bikini. "I'd risk it."

She rolls her eyes at my comment. "Well, how about I wear it this once." she adds, sucking in her teeth in contemplation and sadness, "since I won't be able to wear it much longer, anyway."

"Oh yeah?" I cross my brows, not sure what she's getting at. "And why's that?"

"Because once my stomach gets big, I'll be the one wearing a bag,"

Slowly, I uncross my arms. Francine's hands are still around my neck and she leans forward hard making us both rock back. I grab her waist, thinking about the past few mornings she hasn't felt well and her increase in appetite - especially on wing night.

"You havin' my baby?" I ask, afraid that I misunderstood.

"Yes," she whispers, those pink lips twitching up into a wide smile.

I'm either going to pass out or throw up. So, I grab the nape of her neck and kiss her hard until I'm feeling better and grounded instead.

"I take it that means you're happy?" She pants through a giggle, her face glowing.

"I'm happy. I'm damn over the moon!" I answer honestly. Certainly, she can feel my heartbeat thumping right out of my chest. "But you're both still going to change before we leave!"

Francine kisses my cheek and lets go of my neck, sliding her hands down my stomach wantonly until she reaches the top of my pants. She's looking at me like a damned sex vixen when she pulls me forward using my jeans, kisses my chin, and goes to clean up the mess Lou Lou's made with her pool toys.

And when we're packed up in the Eagle, on our way to the park, I look over at my woman in her pink bikini and glance in the rear view at my daughter in her matching pink bikini and mutter, "Jesus, I hope this is a boy."

WAIT! THERE'S MORE!

The story of the ride or die boys in Eddington continues! Keep reading for the first two chapters of *Wren*!

Also By Kris Renee

Wren

The second book of *The Brat Pack* Series is available now!
Never want to miss a book release?
Sign up for the latest news on upcoming novels, sales, and
merch at www.krisrenee.net!

CHAPTER ONE
SHOP CLASS

Eddington, Ohio 1968

Tomorrow is Graduation Day.

I told my parents I'm not walking across the stage of Eddington High School. Not because I don't think I deserve to, but because I don't give a shit either way. I get the same piece of paper as everyone else whether I'm there or not. And my parents are too busy fighting with each other or making up in the bedroom to care.

Butch, Kurt, Jax, and I all agreed that we'd rather hang out in Kurt's garage and celebrate with a radio and a keg of beer than be around a bunch of kids that we don't even know. One thing the four of us had in common when we met four years ago - we never really fit in at school. Not until we enrolled in shop class and found each other.

Driving over to Sandy's house, The Doors blasting *Hello, I Love You* on the radio of my grandpa's orange Chevy Chevelle, I'm trying to play it cool. But I think tonight Sandy's gonna finally give in and let us go all the way, and I'm wound up tight.

The amount of time I've spent dreaming about this moment is pretty damn embarrassing. I talk a big game in front of the boys, but I've never done *it*. I've never let anyone get close enough. Honestly, after watching my parents love to hate each other every Goddamn day, I never thought it seemed worth it - the whole relationship thing. Why be miserable year after year for only a few days of happiness sprinkled in there like fucking confetti?

But Sandy's different. I knew it the first time I saw her. She was sitting outside of the Dairy Shack the end of last summer. I'd never seen anyone look so damn perfect. Her long blonde hair was blowing in the wind, while she read her magazine and ate her ice cream cone. Not giving a shit what was going on around her. Just sittin' at that table in the grass with her legs crossed. Those high blue socks accentuating every inch of her legs and her short plaid skirt riding up her thighs, giving me, and no doubt any other guy that happened to walk by, a gorgeous view. But the pearls sitting on top of her baby blue collared shirt and sweater in the same shade are what really told me she was out of my league.

Any girl that matched her shit like that, that woke up every morning and made sure to leave the house looking all put together like that, wouldn't be interested in a guy that spent his time under cars and walked around with automotive oil and grease in his nails.

So, I walked by her and stood in line to order my shake. Turning around to look at her every few seconds. I couldn't help myself. She was like an angel, glowing in the sun. How had I never seen her around before? There's no way I wouldn't have noticed her at some point.

"You're joking, right?" Kurt asked from beside me.

"Hm?" I turned forward, pretending now to know what he was talking about.

"Why the hell not?" Wren said. "Shoot your shot, man!"

I guess I wasn't as sly as I thought with my ogling if the guys picked up on it in just the short walk from the car to here.

"Her name's Sandra," Jax chimed in. "Just moved here a few weeks ago from New York City."

"How the hell do you always know shit about every-body?" Kurt asks. "It's fuckin' creepy, man."

Jax just laughs and shrugs. It's true though. He's like damn Dragnet. Always listening and always watching.

We ordered our drinks and started to head back to Kurt's car. I took one last look at her. She was standing up, wiggling her little skirt back down her thighs. And when she turned around to the big metal trash can to throw away her napkin, the wind kicked up and blew her magazine right off the table and across the field next door.

I didn't hesitate. I saw it for the golden opportunity it was and ran after the colored pages tumbling over the grass.

When I caught it, I looked at the cover real quick before I rolled it up in my hand and walked right up to her. It was definitely one of those fashion magazines. The lady on the cover looked French and shit.

Thank you!" She said, standing next to her table and watching me approach. "I never would have caught it in time!"

"No problem." I gave her the glossy book and pocketed my hands into my jeans to try to hide the stains. "Looks fancy."

"What?" She asks at the same time I nod my chin to the magazine. "Oh! Yeah. It's all my mother reads."

"You looked pretty into it," I told her. Sort of admitting that I'd been watching her.

She giggled, "Yeah, I guess. I just brought it along so I wouldn't look so sorry sitting here by myself. Silly really."

"I get it," I tell her. "But a good-looking girl like you should have no problem finding someone to take you out for ice cream."

Her face gets red at the compliment and she looks down at her blue shoes. Damn, she's cute.

"My name's Wren Scout."

She lifts her head and her hair blows around in the wind. I watch her thin, delicate finger tuck the strands behind her ear and then she puts her hand out, "Sandra. Sandra Roberts. But everybody calls me Sandy."

Shit. I hesitate pulling my hand out of my jeans. She looks almost wounded at the slight, and awkwardly starts to put her offered hand down. I reach out and grab her small hand in mine. "I'm sorry. I just didn't want to get your pretty hand dirtied up by touching mine," I explain as I watch her look down to my dirty fingers.

"I'm in shop and work down at the garage on the weekends." I explained. Feeling self-conscious for the first time in my life about what I'm wearing, what I look like, and how old my boots are. I mean, you can't go wrong with white shirts and jeans, but I feel inadequate next to someone so beautiful.

"You're in shop?" Sandy asked, confused.

"Uh, yeah. Shop class. At school?"

If I'm seeing right, she almost looks embarrassed. "Oh. Yeah. I've never heard of it. I don't go to school. I have a private tutor that comes to my house."

Yep. She's out of my league. I don't have a chance in hell.

Not sure what else to say, I pocket my hand again and rock back on my feet. I suppose now's as good a time as any to end this conversation and get back to the boys. It's not like she'd ever go out with me.

As if she picked up on my decision to leave, she takes a step forward and says quickly, "But I'd love to hear more about it!"

I can't help but chuckle a little and raise my brows. "You'd like to hear more about shop class?"

"I'd love to!" She answers excitedly. "I mean, if you'd like to tell me about it sometime?"

Having a feeling she's glorifying a job that ain't glorious in the least, I break it to her slow. "I spend my time underneath dirty cars fixing them. I don't think that a girl like you would be interested in hearing about a job like that."

"Why not?" She asks, sounding offended. "For every new machine that's made there has to be someone that knows how to fix it!" Putting her hands on her hips, she adds, "And to be that someone, someone that other people rely on? Well, there's no shame in that!"

I've had my share of scuffles. And I've been knocked on my ass a few less times than I've been the one doing the knocking. But I've never been knocked on my ass by words. Until now.

"That's a real "worldly" way to look at it," I tell her honestly.

She looks at me funny and then laughs. It sounds like music. No shit. Straight out of the radio.

The boys are yelling my name now from Kurt's car. And a whole lot of profanity.

Sandy looks around me to where they're acting like clowns. "I think your friends are waiting for you."

I don't even bother turning around to them. I know what I'll see. "They can wait longer."

Sandy's eyes drift back to mine and she smiles. My heart skips a beat.

"So, uh, do you want to go out with me sometime? Talk shop?" I'm nervous as hell and I sound like an absolute fool.

"Yes!" She yells out. Her cheeks grow bright red, and she says quietly, "Yes. I'd love to."

If I didn't think she'd notice, I'd pinch myself to make sure this is real. I've not asked a lot of girls out, but I know it's not usually this easy.

"Great." I scratch the nape of my neck, trying to figure out what happens next. "Maybe I should get your number?"

"Oh. Um, no." She's biting her lip and her brows are creased. "But I could meet you here? Are you busy tomorrow around the same time?"

I wouldn't care if I had a scheduled meeting with the President of the United States. I'd cancel it to be free tomorrow afternoon. "Sure. That sounds good."

"I'll uh, I'll see you tomorrow then?" I ask, starting to walk backwards towards where my buddies are.

She nods, smiling, "Tomorrow."

And that was it. From that day, I was hooked on Sandy.

I met her at the Dairy Shack the next day. And we talked about cars. And motorcycles. Engines and wheels. Everything I liked, everything I did, she wanted to know about.

She loves watching me work on grandpa's car, she loves listening to me talk about the boys, about school, about shop class. And I love everything about her.

We rarely argue and the more time we spend together, the harder it is to keep our hands off each other. Things have gotten pretty heavy lately, and it's getting more difficult each time to stop before we go too far. And damn. I want to go too far.

Last night, parked between the bushes in the back of the diner parking lot, the windows foggy and her shirt off, she panted against my lips that she was ready. I nearly yelled out and came in my pants from excitement. Until I remembered that I didn't have any rubbers on me.

So tonight, I'm taking her up to the make-out point overlooking Brandywine Falls.

Reaching to my back pocket, for the hundredth time since I left, I check to make sure the condoms I bought earlier are still there. I don't think my balls could survive a replay of what they went through yesterday.

I pull over to the side of the road a few houses down from hers and wait. This is how it has to be since her father would never approve of me. I can't call her. I can't go to her door to pick her up like a proper date would.

Her father is a big-wig businessman. He moved his family to the huge house on the outskirts of Eddington in order to supervise the building of his newest grocery store chain.

Bill Roberts is here until the six stores, scattered throughout the Midwest, are complete. Once they're up and running smoothly, he's moving his family back to their high rise in Manhattan.

It doesn't matter though. As soon as Sandy graduates next year, I'm going to ask her to marry me. And then I won't have to sneak around with my girl anymore. And she won't have to move away.

I only sit in the car a few minutes before I see her walk out the front door and skip down the steps. She's running towards me with her little white sweater in her hands.

CHAPTER TWO
HELL, YES

We've moved to the back seat of the Chevelle.

A Whiter Shade of Pale is playing on the front speakers. Sandy's shirt is off and I've managed to get her bra off too with her help. Who knew those clasps were so damn hard to work with?

She's laying back on the seat, and I'm kissing her soft lips. She tastes like cherries.

"Let's take your pants off," she whispers against my mouth. Hell yes.

I sit back on my haunches and quickly undo the button of jeans. Unzipping the fly, I grab the waistband and my briefs and pull them down at the same time. My cock springs up as soon as it's released.

Balancing on one leg in the cramped space, I throw off my boot and pull my pants all the way off. I do the same on the other side and once I've finished, I look at Sandy spread out underneath me.

Completely naked except for her white panties, I take a good look at the breasts I've felt in my hands countless times in this car. It's dark in here, but her skin is so white it practically glows against the night around us. Her pink nipples are pebbled and hard.

She has a tan line from her swimsuit on her shoulders and her hair is splayed out around her head. When my gaze falls on her face, I see she's looking her fill at my hard dick.

Slowly, I run my hands up the outside of her smooth thighs and when I reach the narrow piece of fabric around her hips, I loop my fingers underneath it and steadily pull it down her legs.

Sandy lifts her ass up and then her legs to make it easier for me to get the panties off.

"You're so beautiful," I tell her, unable to look away from the mound of blonde hair at her pussy. "Are you sure you're ready?"

"Yes!" She pants, rubbing her legs together.

I pick up my pants from the floor of the car and pull out a rubber from the back pocket. My hands are shaking and I try to take a few deep breaths. Ripping the foil open with my teeth, I spit out the torn piece and unwrap the condom. Before I can get it to my dick, my stupid trembling fingers drop it somewhere on the floorboard. "Fuck!"

"What's wrong?" Sandy asks, sitting up quickly at the same time I'm bending down.

Our heads knock together and we both groan, holding our foreheads. "Ow!" She exclaims.

"Shit!" Now I'm shaking like a fucking leaf, I've lost my condom, and my head is pounding. "I dropped it!"

I can't see a damn thing down there. Sorting through our shit, I push around pants, socks, shoes and shirts until I finally find it.

"Aha!" I say loudly, more to myself.

Sandy starts giggling. She's laying back again, her small fingers on her head where we collided, her perfect tits jiggling with her laughter.

If I lost some of my erection because of my jittery unskillfulness, her giggle hardened that right up.

Rolling the condom around my dick, I hover over Sandy's creamy skin. Adjusting my body in the cramped quarters between her thighs so that my cock is right at her entrance. I rest my forearms on either side of her head and kiss her mouth again as I pull my ass forward and push myself into her.

Both of our breaths catch when her tight pussy gives way for my dick to slide all the way in.

"Fuck, baby," I whisper, sinking down on top of her. My entire body is pressing into Sandy's and my cheek is resting hard against her head. The sensation of being inside of her is so intense that I've lost all use of my limbs and muscles.

I stay completely still, trying to concentrate. Attempting to regain my strength and control. But I can't do it. Not with her sweet smell surrounding me and her pussy clamped around my dick like a vise.

Rearing back the slightest bit, I grunt and jerk forward hard once, twice.

My body starts convulsing and I moan, low and long. White stars shoot off behind my eyelids as I come harder than I ever have any before.

I'm certain I must be dead from pleasure until I hear her whisper my name. "Wren, I can't breathe."

Pushing up on my arms with all my strength, I lift my chest off hers and peel my cheek off of her face. With every movement, my dick moves inside of her and spams.

I'm having a hard time making out her face in the shadows. "Are you okay?" I mutter. Barely coherent enough to speak.

"That wasn't what I expected," she said wearily.

Cupping her cheeks, I press my forehead to hers. "I'm sorry. I don't know what happened."

She starts to giggle. "I think we both know what happened."

I squeeze my eyes closed and groan. "You can't laugh like that when I'm still inside you, baby. It's too much.

"Did you like it?" She asks hesitantly. Her breath is warm against my skin.

"No. I didn't like it." I answer, my lips kissing one eye and then sliding over to the other. "I fucking loved it." I run my nose across hers. "I liked it so much that I went and screwed it up for both of us."

I pull my limp dick out of her and she winces, taking a sharp intake of air. "Shit, Sandy! Did I hurt you?" I rear back on my feet and run my hands through my hair.

"I'm okay, Wren." She sits up in the seat, her arm covering her breasts modestly. "I heard it would hurt. I guess I just thought that it would last longer."

Doesn't matter if you're 18 or 58, no man ever wants to hear that. Even if it's said innocently from a sweet, pretty mouth. I clear my throat, "Yeah, it probably should have."

Fuck. No way I'm telling the boys about this.

I start to dig through the pile of clothes to find her stuff. Placing the bra and shirt on her lap, "Do you, ah, do you want me to help you get that back on?" The offer is sincere, but I can't bring myself to look at her.

"No, I've got it." Sandy says quietly as she pushes her arms through the straps and leans forward to latch it in the back.

We get dressed in the close confines of the backseat in silence. I've finished before her, and I don't know what to do with my eyes. I want to look at her - to watch her dress. To tell her how much I love her. And you'd think after what we just did that, I would be able to. But I've fucked everything up so much that I have no fucking clue what to do now.

"I'm done," Sandy says. There's a tremor in her voice.

I nod my head and rub my hands against my jeans. "I guess we should climb up and head out."

The first to take my seat in the front, I reach under the steering wheel where the keys are still dangling from the ignition and start up the car.

When Sandy squeezes between the two seats, her smell follows her and I take in a deep inhale. She settles herself and clasps her hands together in her lap, her head down and her hair forming a curtain around her face.

Giving her a small smile, positive that she must hate me, I ask her if she's ready to go. She shakes her head up and down before turning to look out the window. Fuck. I messed up so bad.

Sandy stares out the window the rest of the way back into town. And by the time I pull the car off to the side of the road to drop her off, I feel like I'm going to be sick.

Desperate, I plead my case. "I know I messed up. I didn't mean to hurt you. I'd *never* hurt you on purpose. I love you too much."

I'm not even finished with the "much" before Sandy's

flying through the air and onto my lap. Her blonde hair is on my shoulder and she's kissing all over my face. "I was so worried you were upset with me." Her lips are dotting every inch with soft pecks, and I can feel the wet tears leaking from her eyes on my skin.

"What? Are you crazy?" My hands wrap around her throat and I use my thumbs to push her chin up. "You were perfect! So, fucking perfect!" My brows draw down. "God, baby. I thought I -" I can't even finish. The idea of losing her is too much.

"Never." She answers seriously, knowing what I was going to say. "I love you, too, Wren. So much."

I look into her big green eyes, illuminated in the glow of the streetlights. I'll never feel this way for anyone else. Sandy Robertson is my beginning and my end.

"Can we try again tomorrow?"

I bark out a relieved laugh. "Hell, yes," I answer, pulling her to me and kissing her again.

About The Author

Kris Renee is currently loving TikTok, baking, and kissing books.
Her favorite kind of hero is a little bit alpha-hole and a whole lotta tender heart; you know – the strong and silent type.
Kris lives in the Midwest with her husband, their eight children, and two stinky dogs.
She is a lover of dangly earrings, reading, decorating, and peanut butter.
Kris spends summers camping with her big family in their travel trailer (pulled by their 15-passenger van).
She enjoys visiting as many State and National Parks as possible on their trips, roasting s'mores over the campfire every night, and convincing her husband to stop at every ice cream and souvenir shop along the way!
Find Kris on TikTok: @krisreneeauthor Instagram: @krisreneeauthor Facebook: @KrisReneeAuthor
Or visit www.krisrenee.net for fun behind-the-scenes information, new book releases, book sales, and more!

Made in the USA
Las Vegas, NV
26 August 2024